How to Love a Rockstar

Cash & the Sinners #2

D.E. Haggerty

A Love for Lexi
About Face
At Arm's Length
Hands Off
Knee Deep
Molly's Misadventures

Chapter 1

Virginia – the shy girl who doesn't appreciate being manipulated by her friend

11 YEARS AGO

Virginia

I notice Dylan walking my way down the hallway and duck my chin until my hair covers my face. It's possible I also lean forward until my head is nearly inside of my locker.

Indigo bumps my shoulder. "You should ask him out."

I gasp. "Me? Ask him out? Have you lost your mind?"

Dylan is one of the cool kids in our senior class. He plays guitar and is in a band with Indigo's boyfriend, Cash. Whereas, I'm the shy girl who spends most of her time in the library studying. Cool kid and shy girl do not go together.

"It's the Sadie Hawkins dance this weekend. Girls ask the boys out. It's tradition."

I know it's tradition. I also know, "I'm not asking him out."

"I happen to know he doesn't have a date," she sings. "And the band doesn't have a gig."

"He's probably waiting for Britney to ask him."

Britney is the head cheerleader. She's blonde and bubbly and the most popular girl in school. She also believes her mission in life is to torture me.

One more year. One more year. And then I can escape this high school and this town for good.

"Hey, Indigo," Dylan greets as he passes us.

I sigh. He's just so darn cute. His blond hair is shaggy and in need of a cut causing him to spend half the day flicking his head to get the hair out of his eyes. Thank goodness. Because I could gaze into those ocean blue eyes all day long. Assuming I could ever actually meet his gaze.

He reminds me of a typical surfer boy. Which makes sense since we live in San Diego. Except he's not wearing board shorts and flipflops. He's wearing worn jeans with holes in the knees and a t-shirt from the band the *Foo Fighters*. His vibe doesn't say beach, it screams bad boy.

"Don't you have a study period now?" Indigo asks and brings me out of my daydream of being serenaded to by Dylan. Never mind Dylan isn't the singer of the band.

"I do. I'm off to the library. Do you need me to research something for you?"

"No, silly. I need you to ask Dylan to the Sadie Hawkins dance."

"What part of 'never going to happen' are you having diffi-culty understanding?"

She chuckles. "All of it."

"Indigo," I grumble.

Indigo has been my best friend since Britney and her friends decided it would be fun to trip me the first week of our freshman year. I ended up sprawled on my face on the floor with my books scattered throughout the hallway.

Indigo helped me pick up my things and gave Britney a piece of her mind. It was glorious. I love her like a sister but I don't enjoy being ordered around.

"I haven't hung out with him much since Cash and I haven't been dating long, but Dylan seems like a nice guy. He's not the same as these other assholes in this school."

Nice guy and guy willing to date the mouse no one notices unless they need someone to cheat off of in calculus class are not the same things.

I don't tell Indigo what I'm thinking, though. She'll get mad at me for putting myself down. It's not putting myself down if it's the truth but it's a waste of breath trying to explain that to her. She doesn't listen anyway.

The girl may be my best friend, but she's also stubborn. Just ask our English teacher Mr. Jarrod what happened when he gave Indigo a B on an essay in our junior year. Spoiler alert – she got an A in English class last year.

"I'm not asking him out," I insist. I'm not asking any boy out. I'll skip the humiliation for the day, thank you very much.

"Tell you what."

Uh oh. Those words are never the bearer of good news.

"If you ask him out, I'll go with you to that exhibition you've been raving about."

My eyes widen. "You will? It's at the Getty."

She shrugs. "Sure. I can drive."

I study her. She's not cracking her knuckles or shuffling her feet. In other words, she's not lying. This is awesome. I'm dying to go to the William Blake exhibition, but the Getty is in LA and I have no way to get there. I don't have a car and money is tight.

"But you have to ask Dylan to the dance."

"He's just going to say no."

"You don't know until you ask." The bell rings. "Gotta go." She doesn't rush off, though. Nope. She stares me down. "Ask him."

I scowl at her back as she saunters off. Easy for her to say. She's dating the coolest kid in school. Meanwhile, the only date I've gone on was with a football player who wanted me to do his English Lit homework for him. He didn't get an A in English last year.

I slam my locker shut and make my way to the library. Enough about boys. I have a history test I need to study for. Good grades are my ticket out of this town.

"Hey!"

My heartrate increases at Dylan's shout. But I ignore him. He's not trying to catch my attention. Why would he?

"Hey, you!"

I slow and scan the hallway. It's empty except for the two of us. Is he actually speaking the me?

I stop and wait for him to catch up to me.

"M–m–me?" I squeak.

"Indigo said you wanted to speak to me."

How dare Indigo? She knows I would never ask Dylan out and yet she sends him over to me?

"At least, I think it was you," Dylan says when I don't speak because I'm too busy figuring out ways I can kill my best friend without getting caught burying her body.

Dang it. What to do? I can walk away. I'd be humiliated but what's new? Or, I can ask him out and he'll say no. In which case, I will also be humiliated. It appears humiliation is the special of the day. It often is.

I glance up at him from beneath my lashes. He's gazing down at me in confusion.

"Do you need help?" he asks.

"Um, no." I blow out a breath and force myself to speak the words. I can do this. I'm shy not a coward. "Do you want to go to the dance with me?"

He shoves his hair out of his eyes. If I weren't a scaredy-cat, I'd gaze into those ocean blue eyes instead of ducking my chin to study the floor. Trust me. The floor isn't very interesting. I've spent enough time studying it.

"I'm sorry. I didn't catch what you said."

Probably because I mumbled. I wince. I know better than to mumble.

I clear my throat. "Do you want to go to the dance with me?"

Now he probably thinks I have a speech impediment considering how slow I spoke. Gah! I'm such an idiot. Why can't I be a normal girl and speak with a normal voice at a normal tempo?

"The dance this Saturday?"

I nod.

"Sorry, I can't."

His phone beeps and he glances down at it and winces. Without another word, he rushes away. Meanwhile, my face is hot enough to set off the fire alarm.

I creep into the library and find a spot in the back away from everyone where I can wallow in my humiliation alone.

Never again. I will never ask a boy out again. And I certainly won't crush on Dylan – the 'nice guy' – anymore.

Chapter 2

Dylan – a rockstar about to be hit by lightning

PRESENT DAY

Dylan

I stretch my neck as I wake up. The muscles in my lower back spasm. Ouch. What the hell did I do last night?

I scan the room and realize I'm laying on the floor. Next to me is Fender. Gibson and Jett are at our feet while Cash is in the bed. The band's all here.

We must have fallen asleep in Cash's room after working on the new song all night. I smile. Last night was exactly like old times when we used to gather in the bedroom of my apartment and play music while talking shit about all the crazy things we'd do once we had money from making it big.

Making it big was always the dream. But I never thought *Cash & the Sinners* would actually become a record-breaking band that tours the world and has fans stalking us into toilet stalls at concert venues.

It's been a wild ride but we need a break before we burn ourselves out. We're supposed to be enjoying a year off now. Instead, we're in the tiny town of Winter Falls in Colorado recording our new album because Cash discovered his biological family lives here.

When he found out his ex Indigo was here as well, I knew we wouldn't be going anywhere for a while.

Jealousy burns in my stomach and I rub a hand over it. Not jealousy over Cash finding his family. I've got my mom and sisters. But Cash and his ex, Indigo? Who won't be an ex much longer if Cash has anything to say about it?

I'm ready for the kind of love they have. Too bad I'm surrounded by fans who are too enamored by my fame and dollar signs to get to know the real me.

Enough of this melancholy. I get to my feet and go in search of a bathroom. Once I finish my business, I make my way to the kitchen. I need coffee.

As soon as the smell of coffee permeates through the house, my bandmates tumble into the kitchen.

"What's for breakfast?" Fender asks but doesn't wait for an answer before opening the refrigerator.

Fender is the bass player of *Cash & the Sinners*. He's also a giant who's always hungry.

Cash slams the door on him. "No raiding the kitchen."

Cash is the lead singer of *Cash & the Sinners*. He also thinks he's our leader. But no one can keep these clowns under control.

"But I'm hungry." Fender's stomach growls in agreement.

"Me too," Gibson says.

"Me three," Jett adds.

Gibson is our rhythm guitar player and Jett is the drummer. They're also the reason Cash can't keep the band under control.

Gibson is a charmer who enjoys making women fall at his feet while Jett is an adrenaline junkie who thought a quick trip to climb Mount Etna while we were on tour in Italy was a good idea. It wasn't.

"I'll get some takeout." Cash settles a glare on each of them. "Behave while I'm gone."

Gibson bats his eyelashes. "I always behave."

"You always snore," Fender corrects.

"I do not snore." Gibson stalks toward Fender.

Cash moves to stand in front of Gibson. "Behave or there will be no breakfast this morning."

Gibson sniffs and backs up. "Fine."

Once Cash is gone, we settle at the kitchen table and I pour everyone coffee. It isn't long before footfalls on the stairs indicate Indigo is on her way downstairs. Not surprising since this is Indigo's grandmother's house. By some weird coincidence, Cash ended up renting the house at the same time Indigo's grandma died and Indigo returned to settle the estate.

"Good morning!" I greet when she enters the kitchen.

She scans the room and narrows her eyes when she realizes the entire band is in her kitchen. "What are you doing here? What are all of you doing here?"

Gibson smirks. "We had a slumber party."

Fender grunts. "We fell asleep working on a song."

Jett sticks his tongue out at Fender. "Where's your sense of adventure?"

"I think you have enough adventure in you for the two of us."

Gibson smirks. "I have a sense of adventure."

The back door opens and Cash strolls in carrying several bags. "Getting takeout in this town is a hassle," he mutters. When he catches sight of Indigo, he smiles. "Good morning, Indy. Sorry about these ruffians. They climbed through my window last night and wouldn't leave."

"Says the man who ate all the potato chips," I complain.

Cash lifts up the bags he's carrying. "I brought breakfast as a peace offering."

"Yes!" Gibson dives at the bags.

Jett snatches a bag from Gibson's hands. "I'm starving."

Cash snaps his teeth at them. "If you ruin Indy's blueberry pancakes, I'm going to kick your asses."

"Blueberry pancakes?" The warmth in Indigo's eyes as she looks at Cash has the flare of jealousy in my stomach reigniting. I ignore it. I refuse to be jealous of two of my oldest friends.

Cash hands her a plate. "I remember they're your favorite."

Everyone settles around the kitchen table to dig into their food.

"Are you guys going to the recording studio this morning?" Indigo asks.

"Nope," Cash says. "Not until this afternoon. If it's okay with you, I want to help you bring those boxes to the library first."

"You don't have to. If you need to work, I understand."

"I'll help, too," I volunteer since I know Cash is going to help no matter what Indigo says. And we really should be in the recording studio. The sooner we finish this album, the sooner we can have a break. "We'll be done in no time and then we can hit the recording studio to record our new song."

Cash kicks me under the table. I glare at him. "Why did you kick me?"

"No reason," he grumbles.

"It's no secret our *new* album will have *new* songs on it."

"Oh no," Gibson whines. "Mommy and Daddy are fighting."

Fender punches his shoulder. "No."

Gibson bats his eyelashes. "No, what?"

Fender doesn't respond. He simply grunts before focusing his attention on his sausage and eggs.

Jett drops his fork and leans back while rubbing his stomach. "I guess I'll have to figure out a way to amuse myself while Cash and Dylan help Indigo."

Jett left to his own devices is never a good idea.

"No way. You'll end up in trouble." I turn to Indigo. "Let me tell you about the time he decided to try magic mushrooms."

We laugh and joke as we eat breakfast. It's like old times. Jett gets mad and storms out of the house when we make fun of him. Exactly like old times.

Except Indigo is now a member of our crew. If only I could find a woman to love who also fits in with my friends.

She sighs as she stands to gather the dishes. "We need to get going. I promised the librarian I'd be at the library by now."

"Gibson and I'll clean up," Fender offers.

"Why did I get roped into helping?" Gibson complains but he takes the dishes from Indigo and begins cleaning up.

Cash and I load the truck up with boxes and we drive to the library. Once we're parked on the square, Indigo jumps out to meet the librarian while Cash and I carry in the boxes.

"Look who I found, Cash," Indigo says when we enter the storage room. "You remember my friend Virginia? She's one of the librarians here."

I glance over and catch sight of the most beautiful woman in the world. She has long brown hair pulled high in a bun on the top of her head displaying her long and elegant neck. A neck I'd love to nuzzle while my hands play with those curves her sweater and short skirt can't hide. Then, I'd rip off those glasses that give me all kinds of ideas about playing the librarian and the naughty patron before I—

Bam! I run smack into the wall. The box I'm carrying topples to my feet, and the books scatter everywhere.

"What's going on back there?" a woman yells.

"Nothing!" Virginia yells back. My little librarian has some lungs on her. I wonder if I could get her to scream in the bedroom. I don't mind putting in the effort. In fact, I look forward to it.

"Keep your voice down!"

Virginia rolls her eyes. "You better get out of here. Gratitude is going to be a bear with all this ruckus."

Cash wipes his hands on his jeans. "We're finished anyway. Good seeing you, Virginia." He smirks at me. "You coming, butterfingers?"

I don't want to go anywhere. I want to spend my morning getting to know my little librarian. When I glance her way, she ducks her head, but not before I notice the frown. Why is she frowning at me? Does she not know who I am?

Wait. Does she not know I'm a rockstar? Intriguing. I can't wait to introduce myself to Virginia, the little librarian. Our stay in Winter Falls is suddenly looking up.

I clear my throat. "Yeah, I'm coming."

But I'll be back my little librarian. You can count on it.

Chapter 3

*V*IRGINIA

"Is Eostare the same as Easter?" I ask my boss Gratitude as we stroll toward Main Street for the festival.

She scowls at me. "How can you not know what Eostare is?"

Because people outside of Winter Falls have no idea what it is, I think but don't say. I know better than to back-talk my boss and landlord. Why did I ever agree to live with my boss while I search for a more permanent place to stay?

Silly me. I thought Gratitude, as the elderly librarian who is retiring, would be welcoming to me as her replacement. Not even close. She resents having to retire. She resents having to hire me. She resents having to train me. She's a big ball of resentment with a gray mop of hair on top.

"I'd never heard of Eostare before today," I admit and wait for her to put on her condescending hat. She's worn it a lot since I came to Winter Falls to become the town's librarian.

Sure enough. She sniffs and her nose lifts in the air as she answers, "Eostre is the fertility goddess of humans and crops.

She mated with the solar god of the spring, Equinox, and nine months later gave birth to a god child."

Winter Falls sure loves pagan stuff. I probably should have read up on pagan festivals before coming to live here, but I was so excited to finally land a position as head librarian, I packed up and moved before the ink on my employment contract was dry.

"And how do we celebrate the mating of the fertility goddess with the solar god?"

Gratitude doesn't answer. She doesn't need to. We round the corner to Main Street and oh my. The street is packed with people. The shop owners have set up booths to sell their wares on the sidewalk, and I can smell all kinds of yummy food. My stomach rumbles in response.

"There's a craft fair in the park if you're interested," Gratitude says before waving at someone and walking away.

A craft fair sounds interesting since I could use some decorations to liven up the apartment I'm moving into next week. I can't wait to get out of Gratitude's house and have my own place. No roommates, no family, no landlord. All mine. All I've ever wanted is a place of my own.

"Virginia! Virginia!"

I scan the area until my gaze lands on Indigo waving me over. I begin toward her until I notice who she's with.

Dylan. The boy who humiliated me in high school. Jerk.

Unfortunately, he's also a handsome jerk. The cute surfer boy from high school grew up into a sexy man. Couldn't he have gained a stomach pouch or gotten a crooked nose from a bar fight? Life isn't fair because Dylan is sexier now than ever before.

Those lean muscles he had in high school are now bulging muscles my fingers itch to touch. Do they feel as hard as they appear? And since when are tattoos sexy? Apparently, if it's a full sleeve tattoo on Dylan's right arm, it is. I shouldn't want to touch them, to feel them with my tongue, but I do. More than I'll ever admit.

I debate pretending I didn't notice Indigo but she cocks an eyebrow in challenge. She knows darn well I don't want to be in the vicinity of the sexy jerk, but she doesn't care. Sigh. The things I do for my friends.

I make my way to her and hug her in greeting.

"Hi, Virginia," Dylan says before Indigo can speak. He reminds me of an eager puppy. Which shouldn't be adorable.

I scowl at him. "Hello, Dylan."

"When are you going to put me out of my misery and go out on a date with me?"

My mouth gapes open. Is he serious? Does he not remember me asking him out in high school? Or how he couldn't say no to me fast enough? And I thought I was humiliated before. Nope. This is a whole new level of humiliation.

"Why would I go out with you? You don't even know who I am."

He wiggles his eyebrows. "Thus, a date to get to know you."

He has got to be kidding me. Does he think I'll jump at the chance to date him since he's a rockstar now? Not happening.

But you want to lick his tattoos, a voice in the back of my mind reminds me. I ignore her. Humiliation trumps licking tattoos no matter how glorious the muscles underneath those tattoos are any day.

"You're an idiot," I mumble before facing Indigo. "I'm going to the craft fair. Let's plan to meet up for coffee soon."

"Yes! It's been too long, girl."

I march off but not before I hear one of the band members yell *burn.* I giggle. Dylan's finally getting a taste of his own medicine. Excellent. It'll do his big fat head good to remember not every woman in the universe wants to throw herself at him.

You want to throw yourself at him, the voice in the back of my mind whispers. I mentally shove my palm in her face to shut her up.

I slow down to do a bit of window shopping at the jewelry store *Bohemian Treasures.* I may also be eavesdropping, but can you blame me? The boy I was obsessed with in high school is getting teased by his bandmates because I said no to a date. I couldn't have written a better script if this were a romance novel.

The ribbing gets cut off when someone screams, "CASH" at the top of her lungs. "I saw Cash from *Cash & the Sinners.* He's here!"

Oh no. The band doesn't have any security in town.

I scoff. "*Cash & the Sinners* wouldn't be in Winter Falls."

The crowd ignores me and I'm jostled as they rush toward the corner where I left Dylan and the others. This is bad. I'm familiar with the nature channel. I know stampedes don't end well for the prey.

I wring my hands as I debate how I could possibly help. Before I can figure out what to do, the police force lines itself up in front of the band to protect them. Local citizens join the line and the crowd calms down.

Soon enough the excitement is over. The crowd disperses but my feet are glued to the ground. I need to know Dylan wasn't injured in the kerfuffle.

It's not because I still want him. He's an idiot with serious memory issues and I promised myself I wouldn't obsess over him anymore. But he's friends with my best friend and she was with him. I want to make sure Indigo wasn't hurt.

I push up on my toes and notice the band milling around. No one appears to be injured and I don't see any blood. Phew. Everyone's fine.

"I have a librarian to locate," Dylan says.

Uh oh. I don't think he's referring to Gratitude. I scurry inside the jewelry store where I wait until he saunters past on the sidewalk.

"Personally, I wouldn't run away when a sexy rockstar wants me," a woman says.

"There's more to the story."

She grins. "There always is." She extends her hand. "I'm Rain."

"Virginia," I say as I shake her hand.

"This is going to be fun."

"Fun? What's going to be fun?" What in the world is she talking about?

She chuckles. "Enjoy the ride."

Enjoy the ride? What ride? Is she referring to my future?

"Are you a fortune teller?" I wouldn't be surprised to find one in Winter Falls.

"Nope." She peeks out of the windows. "The coast is clear." She motions to the jewelry around the store. "Unless you want to buy something."

"Um." I bite my lip.

She barks out a laugh. "Get out of here, Virginia Hale."

I don't bother asking how she knows my last name and hurry to the door.

"And don't forget to tell your man I stock engagement rings," she hollers after me.

I trip on air and have to steady myself on the door before I end up flat on my face. *My man? Engagement ring?*

The woman might not be a fortune teller but she is crazy. Note to self: *Bohemian Treasures* is not a safe hiding place.

Chapter 4

Shock – how you feel when you discover who's living across the hallway from you

VIRGINIA

"Thanks for agreeing to help," I tell Indigo when I open the door. I frown when I notice she's not alone. She has a whole crowd with her – including *him*.

I scowl. "I didn't realize you were bringing *him* with you."

"Who's she referring to?" Gibson scans the group. "It's me, isn't it?"

He swaggers forward, but Jett shoves him out of the way. "I call dibs."

I wish I could say I don't know who Gibson and Jett are. That I didn't follow Dylan's career for the past eleven years. But I can't. I know exactly who they are. I know who all the members of *Cash & the Sinners* are. With how popular the band is, it's hard not to.

Sure, my inner voice snorts. *You keep telling yourself that.*

"You can't call dibs on a woman," Indy says.

My gaze falls on Dylan. Indy, Jett, and Gibson's voices fade away. Despite the chill in the air, he's wearing a t-shirt highlighting the ink on his arm. I study the ink and notice a few girl's names. Typical rockstar. He probably has a bedpost somewhere full of notches. Good reminder.

"Nobody better harm my rose bushes," Gratitude shouts from inside the house.

"Your rose bushes are safe," I shout back at her.

I wouldn't dare harm her rose bushes. She's difficult enough to deal with at work as it is and I haven't done anything wrong.

"Are you going to stand on my porch all day? I thought you were moving out today."

"I am moving out. I'll be out of your hair soon."

"Do I hear Gratitude the librarian? You live with your boss?" Dylan asks.

I glare at him. "I'm moving out. Or did you forget why you're here? Did syphilis rot your brain?"

"Syphilis? Does syphilis still exist?"

"As much fun as this is," Indigo interrupts, and judging by the twinkle in her eye she does think this is fun. "Let's get you moved."

I motion to the boxes stacked in the hallway. "This is my stuff."

"What about your furniture?" Indigo asks.

"I don't have any. The apartment's furnished anyway."

Once all the boxes are stacked in the truck, I rush back into the house. "One more thing."

I pick up Harry's cage and make sure he's steady before returning outside.

Gibson points at Harry. "What the hell is in there?"

"Let me see." Jett sticks his finger in the cage. "Hey there, what's your name?" He yelps. "It bit me!"

I roll my eyes. "Didn't anyone ever teach you to not stick your finger where it doesn't belong?"

Jett waggles his eyebrows. "I've never had any complaints before."

My cheeks flush. "Um… ah…"

Dylan shoves him. "Don't embarrass, Virginia, asshole."

I glare at him. Who does he think he is? He's not my protector.

"I don't need you to protect me," I mumble.

"Come on, Virginia." Indigo herds me toward the truck. "We'll ride to the apartment. The rest of these jerks can walk."

"I'm not a jerk," Dylan proclaims.

"Just an idiot with severe memory loss," I whisper so no one can hear.

We drive to the apartment building – my new home. My leg jiggles up and down as I wait for Cash to back up the truck.

I can't wait to have my own place. I can decorate however I want. I can let the dishes pile up in the sink if I don't want to clean them. Harry can run around without someone screaming he's trying to kill them. It's going to be awesome.

I jump out of the truck as Dylan and his bandmates arrive.

"I win! I was here first," Jett declares.

Fender shoves him. "Not a race."

"Life is a race, dude. Get with the program."

I groan. "You had to bring them with you?"

Indigo winks. "They're fun."

"You have a strange way of saying annoying."

She nudges me toward the front door. "You go ahead and unlock your new place. I'll deal with these hooligans."

Since I don't want to be any closer to Dylan than I have to be – *liar!* – I immediately agree. "Okay. I'm on the second floor. Apartment 203."

I climb the stairs and unlock my door. I'm certain there's a huge smile on my face. *My place. My place. My place.*

It's taken me eleven years since high school graduation, but it's finally happening. I have a place of my own. Harry wheezes.

"I didn't forget about you, sweetie," I murmur as I set the cage down. I open it up and gather him in my hands.

I sit on the sofa and cuddle him as the guys bring in my boxes.

Indigo collapses on the sofa next to me. "What ya got there?"

"This is Harry, the hedgehog."

"Can I cuddle him?" She reaches for him but I scoot away.

"Harry doesn't enjoy other people cuddling him." It took weeks before I could even pet him after I rescued him.

"No shit. He bit my finger," Jett grumbles.

"And you enjoyed it," Gibson claims.

Jett smirks. "I always enjoy it a bit rough."

Dylan punches his shoulder. "No sex talk in front of the ladies."

I glare at him. Why does he think he's my protector all of a sudden? Considering he doesn't remember me, he can take his protector tendencies and shove them up his rear end.

"How did Harry come into your life?" Indigo asks.

"I found him on my driveway when I came home from work one night. He was injured. I rushed him to the vet and nursed him back to health."

"Can I pet him?" Dylan asks.

What part of 'he doesn't enjoy other people cuddling him' does he not understand?

"He's scared of strangers."

He frowns but steps away without pressing his point. Maybe he isn't a complete idiot after all.

"Is anyone thirsty?" he asks the group.

I tuck my chin into my chest as embarrassment hits me. I should have something to offer the guys for helping me move in but I don't. "I haven't had a chance to get groceries yet."

"No worries. I'll grab stuff from my place."

My nose scrunches. "Your place?"

"Yeah. My place." He points to the apartment across the hallway. "I live there."

Hold on. Hold on. This has to be a mix-up. This can't be true. "You live across the hallway from me?"

He grins. "Yep. Didn't you know your new apartment used to be Gibson and Fender's apartment?"

I rear back. "No, I didn't."

How did I not know this used to be the apartment two of the band members were renting? Dang it. I didn't think to ask questions when the owner rang and said she had an opening. I merely jumped at the chance of having a home.

And now my home is across the hallway from the man I'm trying to avoid. The same man who is not doing me the courtesy of avoiding me.

"Don't worry. We bought you new mattresses," Gibson says.

Fender grunts. "My mattress was fine."

"Because you're a monk."

"I'm not a monk."

"Oh, do you prefer the term celibate?"

Fender growls. "Not fucking every woman who throws herself at me doesn't mean I'm celibate."

Gibson scratches his neck. "It doesn't?"

"In case anyone's wondering, I don't have sex with every woman who throws herself at me either," Dylan declares.

No one asked. I don't care how many women he's slept with. How many fans he's crooked his obnoxiously sexy finger at. Nope. Not caring at all. And not jealous either. Definitely not.

"Me either." Cash plops down on the sofa next to Indigo. "I'm a one woman man."

Jett coughs. "Whipped."

"About those drinks?" Dylan asks again.

How do I tell him I don't want anything to drink and could he please go away? And never show his face again? Why can't I channel those mean girl cheerleaders from high school? Why do I always have to be nice?

You know why.

I ignore my inner voice. If she's not causing trouble, she's hinting at truths I don't want to hear.

Indigo stands. "I'm hungry. Who wants lunch at the brewery?"

She herds the band out of the apartment. Before she shuts the door, she mouths to me, *You owe me.*

If me owing her means Dylan is out of here, I'm happy to be in her debt.

Now to figure out a way to live across the hall from the man without giving into temptation.

Because no matter how upset I am by my high school humiliation, Dylan is still the definition of temptation wrapped up in a sexy rockstar package.

Chapter 5

VIRGINIA

A few minutes after the band leaves, there's a knock on the door. They must be back.

"What did you forget?" Oops. It's not Indigo and the band. It's a group of elderly ladies. "I'm sorry. I thought you were someone else."

"Did she think we were Dylan?" one of the women asks.

"Has Dylan already been in her place?" another asks.

"Of course, he has. This used to be his bandmates' apartment."

"This project is going to be my favorite."

I have no idea who these ladies are and definitely not any idea what they're talking about and I don't think I want to know. I clear my throat to gain their attention. "Excuse me. Can I help you, ladies?"

"Let me introduce ourselves," the one in the front says. "I'm Sage. I'm the leader of the group."

"She wishes," the woman next to her mutters.

"This is Feather, Petal, Cayenne, and Clove." She points to each woman in turn. "Together we're the gossip gals."

"The gossip gals?" I ask. I must have misheard. No one would refer to themselves as a gossip on purpose, would they?

Sage beams at me. "Yes, we know everything going on in town." And she sounds very proud of it, too.

Everything? And they named themselves gossips. I'm starting to worry living in a small town is going to be like those small town romances I'm addicted to where everyone is in everyone's business all the time. I'm torn between excitement and scared out of my mind.

"I still say this is a mistake. We're too early," Feather says.

"I agree. We're not done with Indigo and Cash yet," Cayenne adds.

Done with Indigo and Cash? What exactly are they doing to Indigo and Cash? And do I want to know?

"Pish pash. We can handle two projects at once," Petal claims.

"Excuse me. Projects?" I ask when my curiosity gets the better of me.

"Don't worry about it," Sage says. "We'll handle everything."

"We always do," Cayenne adds.

I hate it when someone tells me not to worry. It's my choice whether I worry or not. And I am worried. Worried these women escaped from a mental health facility and I need to contact the police to return them to safety.

"We're not crazy," Sage says.

She thinks she's reassuring me. She's not, since all crazy people claim they aren't crazy.

"But we are the best matchmakers in town."

"In town?" Feather scoffs. "I think you mean in the state of Colorado."

"This side of the Mississippi?" Clove suggests.

I hold up my hand to stop them. "Matchmakers? I don't need a matchmaker." I certainly don't want anyone dictating my life. I am done with letting someone run roughshod over my life, thank you very much.

"Who's this?" Feather asks instead of answering my question.

I skim a hand over the back of my hedgehog. "This is Harry."

"He's adorable. Can I hold him?" Cayenne doesn't wait for an answer before reaching for my pet. I retreat a step.

"He's afraid of strangers."

"We're not strangers," Cayenne claims. "We're friends you've never met before."

Sage snorts. "No repeating bumper stickers."

Cayenne gasps. "Bumper stickers? I do not have a gas guzzling, environment ruining car and you know it."

Based on the Eostare festival, I thought Winter Falls was famous for hosting pagan festivals throughout the year. It's not. Nope. The town's claim to fame is being the first carbon neutral town in the world. Anything the town deems harmful to the environment is banned – food delivery, plastic bags, cut flowers, and cars with internal combustion engines to name a few.

I'm not bothered by the ban on cars, since I don't have one. And why would I need one now? I can walk to the library in less than ten minutes. It's ideal. Or, it will be, as soon as Gratitude actually retires and I can start to implement some changes.

"I've certainly never owned a gas guzzler before," Clove claims, causing an argument to break out amongst them.

This is the perfect opportunity to retreat. "It was lovely meeting you ladies," I say as I begin to close the door.

The arguing immediately stops and Sage wedges her foot in the door to stop me. "We're not finished, young lady."

"You need to fill me in since I have no idea what we're doing."

"I told you we shouldn't be mysterious," Petal says.

Sage snorts. "Because you want to give candles to the participants in the project."

"Candles?" I ask. "Candles are nice."

Petal grins. "You're going to love my candles. I make them myself with all-natural ingredients."

"All of her candles are sex candles," Feather adds.

"Sex candles?" I must have misheard. This woman who's old enough to be my grandmother does not make sex candles. No way.

"Yes." Petal nods. "I have sex candles for all your bedroom needs. Wax play, massage, whatever you need."

I inch backwards. "I don't have a boyfriend. I don't need any sex candles."

She smiles. "Thus, the project."

Project? Matchmakers? Are they saying what I think they're saying? Oh no. I don't think so.

"No. I don't need a matchmaker to find a boyfriend."

"She's adorable," Sage says. "She thinks she has a choice in the matter."

"Excuse me. I do have a choice in the matter." I am done with people telling me what I can and cannot do.

Sage pats my arm. "I don't mean you have no choices. I mean destiny has already decided."

"Destiny?" I'm rethinking notifying the police. Will they flee before they arrive? Should I invite them in and keep them here until the police come?

Cayenne points to my face. "She has the 'they're crazy, maybe I should phone the police'- look on her face."

"I thought after she met Rain, she'd be more open to the idea of destiny." Clove shrugs. "Some people struggle against their fate."

"Speaking of fate," Sage begins, "will you stock more BDSM books once you're the librarian?"

"Um…" I feel my face warm. Discussing my non-existent sex life was bad enough but now we're discussing BDSM? Eek!

"There's no reason to be embarrassed," Feather says. "Sex is perfectly natural. And sexy books are the best."

"She picks out the books for our sexy book club," Petal explains. "In fact, you should join us."

"We meet once a month at the bookstore, *Fall into a Good Book*. Have you been there yet?" Clove asks.

Have I been to the one and only bookstore in town? Of course, I have. I love books. It's kind of a prerequisite to my profession as a librarian.

"Book club is fun, although we've yet to find a man who's willing to strip for us," Clove mutters.

I nearly swallow my tongue. I must have misheard. Why do I always feel as if I'm mishearing these ladies? "Strip for you?"

"To liven things up. We don't have a strip club in town and Juniper won't allow us any sexy movies on movie night."

Feather leans close to whisper, "She says they're porn."

Sage crosses her arms over her chest. "And after we got her together with her movie star husband, too. Where's the appreciation?"

I have no idea what they're talking about and I don't want to. I clear my throat. "I should make myself clear. I don't need a matchmaker. I don't need a boyfriend. I want a chance to settle into my new job and new home."

"You don't want a boyfriend? Not even Dylan?" Sage asks.

In an ideal world where I'm not a librarian, he's not a rockstar, and he remembers me from high school, maybe I'd want Dylan as a boyfriend. Okay, fine. I'd jump at the opportunity.

But we're not living in an ideal world. And Dylan still doesn't remember me from high school. If I'm not worthy of being remembered, I'm not girlfriend material.

Yes! You are! The voice in the back of my mind insists.

Clove smirks. "She's considering it. I can tell."

I am not. I'm not considering Dylan kissing me. Would his lips be soft? They look soft. And I'm definitely not considering Dylan touching me. Flutters erupt in my stomach and warmth spreads over my body as I imagine his hands on me.

"This is excellent. This will be my favorite project," Petal claims, and brings me back to reality where mousy librarians do not date rockstars.

"My love life is not a project," I argue.

Sage pats my arm. "Don't you worry. We'll make sure the betting doesn't get out of control." She snaps her fingers. "Gossip gals move out."

Feather rolls her eyes. "She thinks she's a military general."

Despite her words, the rest of the group follow Sage as she marches down the hallway.

"What bets?" I shout after them. They pretend not to hear me and continue on their way.

I shut the door and lean against it. Great. On top of resisting Dylan who now lives mere feet away from me, I now need to worry about a bunch of old ladies trying to match me with him.

So much for Winter Falls being a peaceful place to live.

Chapter 6

Bandmates — similar to family members except you go to jail if you kill one

DYLAN

I whistle as I stroll through Winter Falls on my way to *Bertie's Recording Studio.* Things are looking up. Cash has his muse back and is writing music again. Which means the band can record our album and our producer will get off our back.

And Virginia is now living across the hallway from me. Since she's extremely shy and shot me down once already, it won't be easy to convince her to date me, but I'm a patient man.

I enter the studio and notice I'm the last to arrive. Our producer, Stan, is already here as is Rob, the studio engineer, and the rest of the band.

"I'm surprised you're on time," I say to Cash.

He groans. "Indy is an elementary school teacher. She's up at the crack of dawn."

Gibson grins. "I didn't get home until the crack of dawn." He smirks. "Ask me where I was."

There's no need to ask him where he was. The answer's obvious – he was with a woman. He fancies himself a charmer. Manwhore is more like it.

"Have you slept with the entire population of Winter Falls?" Cash asks. "I am not dealing with townswomen who are angry because you've led them on."

Gibson gasps. "I would never misrepresent myself to a woman. I can't believe you would think otherwise." He clasps his chest as if he's been injured.

"It wouldn't be the first time," I point out. "Remember the woman in Kansas City? You gave her a ring and she thought you were engaged."

Gibson rolls his eyes. "It was a plastic ring I won at the fair. How was I supposed to know she was crazy?"

"Maybe if you got to know the women you sleep with, you'd figure out if they're crazy or not before they chase after the tour bus without any clothes on."

Gibson smirks. "And miss the bouncing boobs?"

Cash growls and I step in between them before fists can fly. It wouldn't be the first time. Being glued to each other 24/7 for months on end during concert tours can be trying even when you are the best of friends.

"Enough," I order.

"It's not my fault Cash is taking out his lack of getting laid on me," Gibson says.

Cash snaps his teeth at him. "Don't you dare speak about my sex life with Indy again."

I place my palm on Gibson's chest and push him away. "I said enough."

"Uh oh. Daddy's mad," Jett whines.

I glare at him and he smirks at me. He's sitting on the sofa next to Fender who's eating a stack of pancakes.

"I thought Winter Falls didn't do takeout."

Fender grunts and continues to eat his pancakes. What he doesn't do is answer my question. The big guy isn't much of a talker.

"He made a deal with the diner. As long as he brings the dishes and silverware back, they'll wrap up his food in paper bags he is under the strictest of orders to recycle," Jett explains.

"Put the pancakes away. Time to get down to business," Cash orders.

Fender shoves the last of the food into his mouth before standing. He doesn't say a word as he picks up his bass.

"What song do you want to begin with?" I ask.

Cash doesn't get the chance to respond before Jett squeals, "Where are my sticks?"

I groan. "Gibson, if you stole Jett's sticks again, I won't stop Cash the next time he wants to pummel you to the ground."

Gibson snorts. "He can try."

"Oh wait," Jett calls, "here they are."

But he's not holding his sticks in the air. It's an airplane. A Lego airplane.

"Watch this!" He throws the plane to the ground and it breaks into hundreds of pieces. "Boom! Crash and burn. This is Dylan's love life."

Gibson hoots. "Burn!"

Cash chuckles. "You can't deny it's true."

I shrug. I might have crashed and burned with Virginia once, but our story isn't written yet. I have the feeling my little librarian is worth the wait.

"I'm impressed, Jett. You put together a Lego airplane. How much time did you need?" I ask.

Jett shrugs. "It's not as if I have anything else to do."

Shit. A bored Jett is trouble waiting to happen.

Fender grunts. "I don't give a crap if you're bored. If you riffle through my underwear drawer again, I'm throwing you off the roof."

"Don't be so sensitive. It's not as if I haven't seen your underwear before."

Fender stands and begins stalking toward Jett.

"Does anyone want to hear my new song?" Cash asks and Fender stops.

Cash clears his throat and begins to sing.

In the crowded room, she's the queen,

A distant star, the coolest scene.

I try to speak, but she turns away,

Lost in the rhythm of the games she plays.

Apparently, it's make fun of Dylan Day. Whatever. "Haha. Very funny."

"There's more," Cash claims before singing again.

She ignores me like a faded song,

Lost in the noise, I'm moving along.

A wall of silence, a distant stare,

I'm drowning in the depths of her cold, cold glare.

Virginia's glare isn't cold. It's hot. Burning hot. She pretends to not want me but I know she does. I just need to figure out what's holding her back.

"Is this the new song?" Stan asks.

"Nope!" Jett shouts. "It's an ode to the burning embers of Dylan's sex life."

"You know what we should do?" Gibson asks and I consider tackling him since whatever he's going to say is certain to piss me off.

"We should make a scoreboard and keep track of how many times Dylan crashes and burns with Virginia," he suggests.

"Do you think there's a Guinness Book of World Records category for how many times a man is rejected by a woman?" Jett asks.

"Let's ring them." Gibson digs his phone out of his pocket.

Fender grunts before setting his bass down and returning to the sofa where he opens another bag of food containing a plate of sausage and bacon.

"I'm starving," Cash complains before reaching for a sausage. He pauses when Fender glares at him. "Who wants breakfast?"

"Didn't you eat at home?" I ask him.

He smirks. "No time."

I shake my head. He's lucky Tweedle Dee and Tweedle Dum aren't paying attention. The shit they would give him.

"Let's hit the diner. Those pancakes smelled amazing."

"What about recording?" I ask.

He motions to Gibson and Jett. "They're going to be busy for a while."

"I could stop them."

He chuckles. "And give up on the fun?"

"I'm beginning to think I didn't give you a hard enough time when you were chasing Indigo."

He slaps me on my back. "Too bad, brother, because it's your turn now."

I'm not bothered by his words. I'm happy for it to be my turn. I've always been a one-woman man but between recording and touring, there hasn't been enough time to meet a woman who isn't after me because I'm a rockstar.

But now there is. We're in Winter Falls for a while. Cash made a deal with our producer to give us some time off after we finish this album. Time we desperately need to decompress.

Time I plan to use to convince Virginia to give me a chance. The shy librarian who doesn't give a damn about my rockstar status is perfect for me. She doesn't know it yet. But she is.

"You coming, Fender?" Cash asks as we exit the studio.

Fender grunts before standing to follow us.

"Wait for us," Jett shouts.

"We can't miss it if Dylan makes another attempt," Gibson adds as he joins us on the sidewalk outside the studio.

"And here I thought I was bored." Jett smirks. "Watching Dylan crash and burn can never be boring."

"I hope you picked up those Lego pieces," I say.

He throws an arm around my shoulders. "You're funny." In other words, he didn't.

"It's not Rob's job to clean up after you. He's the sound engineer, not the cleaner."

"What do we have here? Is it the library?" Jett uses his hold on my shoulders to stop me on the town square where the library is located. I shove him off of me and continue down the sidewalk.

"Bummer. It's not open yet," Gibson whines. "I guess we're having a long breakfast."

"We're never going to finish this album," I mumble.

"The longer we take to finish the album, the longer we can stay in Winter Falls." Cash winks at me.

"I totally didn't tease you enough when you were chasing after Indigo."

"Nope."

My bandmates are annoying, but I can handle their ribbing. As long as Virginia is in my arms at the end of it. The little librarian won't be able to resist me forever.

Chapter 7

Pizza – a yummy tool used by matchmakers to carry out their sneaky plans

VIRGINIA

"Have a lovely evening," I say goodbye to the patron before ushering her out of the library and locking the door.

It's the first time Gratitude has allowed me to close up without her watching over my shoulder and criticizing every single thing I did. Progress! Finally! Considering she's supposed to retire in a month, it's also about dang time.

I switch off the lights before throwing my arms out and twirling around in circles in front of the circulation desk. "Yes! Yes! Yes!"

My dreams are finally coming true. My own apartment with no annoying family or roommates? Check! A job as the head librarian? Check! A hot guy to call my own?

I come to a screeching halt. Where did that thought come from? I don't need a hot guy. I don't need a guy at all, but if I did need a guy he wouldn't be hot. Average height and average looks is the way to go. No need to worry he's out banging all of his fans.

I slap my forehead. *Enough! Enough, Virginia!* I need to stop obsessing over Dylan. It's ridiculous.

I hurry through the closing checklist and make my way out of the rear exit of the library. My stomach rumbles as I pass *Moon's Diner,* but I don't stop. I can't be eating out every day if I want to save money to buy a house.

The idea of owning my very own house has my hunger disappearing and my stomach tingling with excitement. According to my plan, I should be able to save enough for a down payment by the time I'm thirty-two.

I slow and scan the area when I reach my apartment building. It's been a good day. I don't want a run-in with the sexy rocker to ruin it.

When I don't notice Dylan or any of his bandmates, I unlock the door and climb the stairs to the second floor. I peer around the corner before entering the hallway. Phew. The hallway's empty. I rush from the stairwell to my door.

"There you are!"

Dang it. I wasn't quick enough. Maybe I should take up jogging in my spare time. A bit of interval training to prepare me for short bursts down the hallway.

I force a smile on my face and greet Sage, "Good evening."

"We brought you dinner." Petal lifts the plate she's holding and I sniff. Pizza. I love pizza. My mouth waters at the scent of mozzarella cheese and pepperoni.

"But you have to promise to return the plate when you're finished," Sage says.

"Of course!" I can't help but wonder if they're up to something. No one brings a pizza by without an ulterior motive. Or is this small town living?

I choose to believe this is the gossip gals being neighborly. I will not read into everything everyone says and does. I'm done with the portion of my life where I constantly worry about ulterior motives. I have been for a decade.

I clear my throat. "Do you want to join me?"

"I need to get back to the police station," Sage says.

My eyes widen. "The police station?"

"I'm the police dispatcher." Thank goodness.

"And I have a book calling my name," Petal says.

They wave as they walk toward the stairwell.

I juggle the plate as I open the door. Could this day get any better?

I drop my purse on the floor before placing the pizza on the coffee table. I'm grabbing napkins and a plate when there's a knock on the door.

I peer through the peephole and scowl. What is Dylan doing here?

"I know you're in there."

I sigh before opening the door. "What do you want?"

He grins and my knees go all wobbly. It's not enough he has those brilliant blue eyes? He has to have an adorable dimple, too? A dimple I want to taste with my tongue while exploring the smooth skin of his face with my fingers. I fist my hands before they decide to disobey me and reach for him.

"The gossip gals stopped by. They made a pizza for us."

"A pizza for us?"

He points to the plate on the coffee table. "I believe I found the pizza."

"Why didn't they tell me we're supposed to share it?" I sound as if I'm pouting. Probably because I am. I planned to save the leftover slices for lunch tomorrow. Maybe for dinner, too.

"I don't know but my mouth is watering. It smells delicious." As if on cue, his stomach growls.

Dang it. I don't want to be near Dylan – *liar!* – but I can't let him go hungry.

"Interfering gossip gals and their matchmaking," I grumble before opening the door wide and motioning Dylan inside.

"Matchmaking?" he asks.

Never mind. I'm not telling the man who's asked me out several times since I arrived in Winter Falls how I believe the gang of five elderly women are trying to push us together. He doesn't need any more incentives. What he needs is to remember what happened in high school.

"Why don't I cut the pizza in two? You can take half back to your apartment." *Awesome idea, Virginia.*

But then Dylan frowns and hurt flashes in those blue eyes that remind me of the ocean on a hot summer day. And now I feel like I'm the jerk.

"I'll get the plates," I mutter.

"I brought beer." He lifts a six-pack I hadn't noticed before in the air. "Damn. I didn't ask if you drink beer. I don't have any wine. What kind of wine do you drink? I'll make sure to buy a few bottles for when you come over."

For when I come over? Someone is getting ahead of himself. Way ahead of himself.

I will not be spending any time in Dylan's apartment. I don't care how my body yearns for him. This is the man who embarrassed me in high school and doesn't even remember! The situation couldn't be any more humiliating.

"Beer's fine."

He grins. "A woman who enjoys beer. Perfect."

I roll my eyes. I'm far from perfect.

I head to the kitchen where I pull out another plate and some napkins before returning to the living room. Dylan is already sprawled on the sofa making himself comfortable.

He picks up the remote. "What movie do you want to watch?"

"Movie?"

"Or we can talk while we eat. Get to know each other. How's Harry today?"

Get to know him better when I'm already having a hard enough time resisting him? Bad idea. "A movie sounds good."

He chuckles as he switches on the television. "Rom-com okay with you?"

I narrow my eyes at him. "You enjoy rom-coms?"

He shrugs as his cheeks turn a slight shade of pink. "I grew up with four sisters. I didn't get much choice as to what movies we watched."

Dylan has four sisters? I didn't know. And I thought I knew everything about him.

"Your sisters are never mentioned in the media."

He smirks. "Have you been checking up on me?"

I glare at him. I am not going to admit to stalking *Cash & the Sinners.* I am not a loser fan girl who follows the band from venue to venue throwing my panties at them while they perform.

"My best friend has been in love with the singer of the band since high school. Of course, I read the media about the band."

The happiness is wiped from his face. Darn it. I didn't mean to sound like a b-word.

"Make sense." He points to the TV with the remote. "Now, what movie do you want to watch?"

I shrug. "Whatever you choose is fine."

"What if you've seen it before?"

"I don't watch many movies."

"You don't?"

I motion toward the bookshelves overflowing with books. "I usually read."

"What kind of books do you enjoy reading?"

I feel my cheeks warm. "Everything."

He places a slice of pizza on a plate and hands it to me. "You weren't thinking everything."

No, I was thinking about all the sexy romance books I enjoy reading. The ones with spicy sex scenes I pretend Dylan is the hero of while I read them. I'm not proud of it but somehow my ideal man always ends up having blond hair and ocean blue eyes.

I shove the pizza in my mouth to avoid answering. While I chew, I nod to the remote control. Dylan sighs but he switches on the television and opens my Netflix app.

"This one is supposed to be funny," he says as he chooses a movie.

He opens a bottle of beer and hands it to me before opening his own bottle and holding it up.

"Cheers," he says as he clinks our bottles together.

I settle into the sofa and concentrate on the movie. I do my best to ignore the man sitting next to me but it's pretty hard to ignore a sexy rockstar. Especially when he smells so good and groans as he eats his pizza.

I need to figure out a way to stop this obsession I have with Dylan. It's not healthy. Especially since I won't give in and date the man. Not when he can't remember how he humiliated me in high school. Has he humiliated so many women, he can't remember all of their faces?

It's hard to believe he's lost count of the number of women he's humiliated. He's been nothing but open and genuine since I met him again in Winter Falls. Maybe he's changed.

A flicker of hope sparks in my chest but I quickly douse it. Rockstar who's used to women throwing their panties at him, remember?

Chapter 8

DYLAN

I chuckle as I glance around *Electric Vibes.* This bar is nothing like the venues we usually play in. And I don't mean the small size. The place is a genuine hippie bar.

The walls are covered in posters from Bob Dylan, *The Beatles, The Doors*, and other popular musicians from the 1960s and 1970s. The tables and chairs are brightly colored and don't match. And the lights are colored giving the room a groovy vibe.

Winter Falls is awesome. I wouldn't mind living here forever. My gaze catches on Virginia hiding in the corner of the bar. Forever with Virginia would be even better.

Cash throws an arm around my shoulders. "You ready to play?"

Hell, yeah, I am. My fingers are tingling with excitement to strum my guitar. To be on stage again. To feel the excitement of the crowd.

"Don't worry. Indy will make sure your girl stays to watch you play." He slaps me on the back before rushing onto the stage. The crowd goes wild.

When Jett, Gibson, Fender, and I follow him, people rush toward us. I scowl when I notice Virginia trying to escape, but Indigo catches her at the door and drags her to stand right in front of us.

"Good evening, Winter Falls!" Cash shouts. "This one's for Indigo, the love of my life."

He nods to Jett who taps his sticks to count us off. As I play, my gaze finds Virginia's and I wink. She rolls her eyes and I grin.

We play five songs, and I maintain eye contact with Virginia the entire time. She'll probably deny it to her dying day but her cheeks are flushed with excitement. I watch as she pushes her eyeglasses up. It's adorable the way those glasses glide down her nose only to be stopped by her time and time again.

I never thought a girl wearing glasses was sexy before. I was wrong. I have an entire playbook of sexy librarian ideas I can't wait to try out with Virginia. Those straight skirts and shirts buttoned to her neck along with her hair piled high on her head are my kryptonite. I want to dirty her up.

"We're going to take a small break," Cash announces.

The second the music stops, Virginia takes off. She makes a beeline for the front door but the crowd presses against her to prevent her from reaching her goal. I drop my guitar when I notice her wrap her arms around her waist. She's getting flustered. Not okay. She should only be flustered when I'm involved.

I jump from the stage to rescue her but she's already pivoted toward the rear hallway and is hurrying to the exit.

"Virginia, hold up!"

She ignores me and keeps moving. My long legs eat up the distance between us. I clasp her shoulder and whirl her around.

"Hey, Virginia." I smile at her in greeting.

"I'm going home."

I can't resist the temptation of her long, elegant neck. I rub circles on her skin with my thumb. It's as soft as I thought it would be. I bet all of her skin is soft.

She gasps and hope sparks inside of me.

"You feel it, too."

She wrenches away from me. "I don't know what you're referring to."

I smirk. "A challenge? I do love a challenge."

"I am not a challenge. I am a woman."

Crap. I said the wrong thing. She probably thinks I view all women as challenges. She'd laugh if she knew how few women I've slept with over the years. Unlike Gibson, I don't enjoy screwing women who want me just because I'm a rockstar.

I hold up my hands. "I didn't—"

She pokes me in the chest. "You view women as a competition you're determined to win. Women aren't games."

"You have the wrong opinion of me. I'm not Jett who treats sex like a drug or Gibson who gets a kick out of charming a woman into bed." And, frankly, I'm a bit hurt she believes otherwise. "I thought we were past this. I thought we were friends."

"Friends?" She huffs. "I'm leaving."

She whirls around but I'm not letting her go until she understands I'm not a manwhore the way my bandmates are. I shackle her wrist to stop her.

She wrenches her hand free. "Do not touch me without my permission."

I immediately retreat a step. I have four younger sisters. I know better than to touch a woman without her permission. "Sorry. It was a mistake." She glares a me and I continue, "I wanted to get a chance to ask you out before you go home."

"Buy a clue, Dylan! I will never go out with you!"

What the hell? I thought we were making progress. We had pizza together the other night and it was nice. We chatted and joked before she fell asleep during the movie. I wanted to pick her up and carry her to her bedroom, but I didn't. I didn't want to overstep my bounds. Which is also why I didn't ask her out that night.

Virginia spins around and stomps to the exit. I catch the door before it can slam shut. She glances over her shoulder at me and scowls.

"Leave me alone!"

I wish I could say I'll leave her alone, but I can't. I have four sisters and a mom. They would light my favorite guitar on fire if they knew I let a woman walk home alone when she's spitting mad. Although, they'd probably destroy my guitar anyway if they knew I was the reason the woman is spitting mad.

"I'm not letting you walk home alone and angry."

She stomps her foot. It's adorable. She reminds me of an angry otter and everyone knows otters get cuter the madder they get. "You're not walking me home."

"I'll stay behind you. You don't have to speak to me, but I need to make sure you get home safe."

Her face softens at my words before it hardens once again. "I don't need you to make me feel safe."

There's obviously a story here. A reason why safety is a hot button for her. I wish I could ask her what happened. What's made her crave safety? Was it her past? Was she not safe?

I push all those questions down. She's not answering any questions from me tonight anyway.

"Won't the band be mad you took off without telling them where you're going in the middle of the concert?"

My bandmates know exactly where I am. Wherever Virginia is. The teasing has barely begun with those assholes. And I could not care less.

I shrug. "They'll be fine until I return."

Her annoyance fills the air until she finally throws her arms up. "Fine. Walk behind me. See if I care."

Oh, she cares all right. But I'm not the idiot who's going to remind her of how much she cares.

She begins marching down Main Street. I let her get ahead a bit before following. Her pert ass bounces up and down as she marches. If she knew how much I'm enjoying ogling her ass, she'd kill me in my sleep.

"Did you enjoy the rest of the pizza?"

Her shoulders slump at my question. She pauses on the sidewalk in front of *Bake Me Happy*. "Thank you for wrapping it up."

Those words cost her. But she said them anyway. My little librarian has a backbone made of reinforced steel.

"You're welcome."

I catch a glimpse of her reflection in the front window of the bakery. She appears defeated. Damn. I don't want to make her feel defeated. I want to lift her up. Show her how fantastic she is.

Apparently, I'm doing a crappy job. Maybe I should phone my sisters for advice. I snort. No. I know better. They'd be on a plane here within hours to snoop on the situation.

"Do you want me to get a golf cart?"

Since Winter Falls is obsessed with the environment, no cars are allowed. Instead, there are golf carts stationed throughout the town. But there is no golf course. Those are apparently bad for the environment.

As I expected, at my suggestion that Virginia's too tired to make it home, she begins marching again. I keep my distance but follow behind her.

We're nearly at the apartment when she whirls around to face me. "Would you please answer your phone? It's driving me batty!"

My phone's been beeping with messages since we left the bar. It's easy enough for me to ignore. It's always beeping with messages. I can tell by the tones, these messages are from my bandmates. I don't need their teasing now.

I dig my phone out and switch off the ringer. "There. Better?"

Her eyes widen. "Aren't you going to check the messages?"

I shrug. "No need. If it was an emergency, they'd call."

"If you're not going to answer your messages, why don't you keep your phone on silent all the time?"

I roll my eyes. "Because the band's assistant would lose her mind if I did."

She scowls at the reminder I'm in a band. Is the band why she has a problem with me? I know Indigo struggles with how famous Cash is.

Do I want a woman who hates my fame? Who can't handle the fans and limelight?

Fame isn't real. And it won't last. Love lasts. The love Cash and Indigo have for each other lasted through eleven years of separation. I want what they have.

"You drive me crazy," she grumbles before starting to march to the apartment building again.

When we arrive at the building, she pauses with her hand on the outside door. "We're here. You can go back to your life again."

I frown. Go back to my life? This is my life.

I'm obviously not going to win any arguments with her today. I don't want to argue at all. No matter how cute she is when she's mad.

I motion to the door. "Get into the building and I'll leave you alone."

She starts for the inside but once again pauses on the threshold. "Thank you for walking me home, Dylan."

And with those softly spoken kind words she reels me back in again. Hook, line, and sinker.

"You're welcome, Virginia. Sleep well."

I wait until she climbs the stairs and is out of view before heading back to the bar. I need to come up with a plan to convince her to give me a chance. But until I do, persistence is the name of the game.

Chapter 9

VIRGINIA

"I can't believe you're making me do this," I whine as Indigo drags me down Main Street. Okay, fine. She's not literally dragging me, but it sure feels like she is.

"Trust me. You'll love yoga. It helps with your flexibility. Super handy if you know what I mean." She waggles her eyebrows.

I pretend to not understand her sexual innuendo. "I guess if it'll help me to reach the top shelf of a bookcase, I'll give it a try."

Indigo bumps my shoulder. "Not what I meant and you know it."

"And you know I have no need to be flexible."

"If you'd let a certain blond rocker into your life, you would."

I glare at her. "Never gonna happen."

"Why don't you tell him what happened in high school?"

"Because reliving the biggest humiliation in my life is not on my agenda." Not to mention how our history is helping me keep Dylan at arm's length.

"You are beyond stubborn."

I snort. "Says the woman who still sends our math teacher hate mail for giving her a B minus in tenth grade."

She sniffs. "Bad reviews are not the same as hate mail. Besides, I deserved an A. A B plus at the very least."

"Stubborn," I mutter.

"Pot, meet kettle." She raises her eyebrows and waits for me to contradict her. I don't disappoint her.

"I am not stubborn. Refusing to do what you want me to doesn't make me stubborn."

She points at me. "You literally just defined stubborn."

"Whatever," I mumble and open the door to the yoga studio, *Earth Bliss*. Doing yoga has to be better than listening to Indigo order me around.

"You came!" a woman with curly blonde hair screams.

"This is Olivia," Indigo introduces. "She's Cash's sister-in-law."

"Future sister-in-law." Olivia waves her left hand, showing off her diamond engagement ring. Her other hand rubs her baby bump.

Envy shoots through me. I want a baby, a family, a husband to love me. I'm hoping Winter Falls, far away from my past and family, is my chance. And I'm not talking about a certain guitar player.

Sure, you aren't.

"Hi!" I wave. "I'm Virginia."

"You're the new librarian." Olivia looks me up and down. "Who knew librarians could be this sexy?"

I duck my chin to hide how pink my cheeks are.

"Livie!" A man scolds from behind her. "Don't embarrass her."

"How is telling someone she's sexy embarrassing?" She motions to the man. "This is Peace, my baby daddy."

He growls. "I told you to stop calling me baby daddy."

She widens her eyes to make herself appear innocent. Something tells me this woman hasn't been innocent a day in her life. "Are you saying you're not the father of this child?"

Peace growls. "You know I am."

She bats her eyelashes. "Then, why are you upset when I call you my baby daddy?"

I giggle. This woman is trouble. The fun kind.

"You laughed! We're going to be best friends now." Olivia pulls me into a hug.

"Thank you?" I say when she releases me.

She winks. "I'm a great friend. Ask Indigo. We're best friends, too."

An alarm sounds. "Time to begin." She rushes off.

"She's the teacher?"

"You try and stop her," Peace mumbles before following after her.

Indigo grasps my hand and leads me toward the front of the class. I dig my feet in. I am not standing in the front row at my first yoga class.

"Stubborn," Indigo mutters as she switches direction.

"Not wanting to do what you want me to do doesn't make me stubborn."

We find two empty spaces in the back of the room right before a gong sounds.

"Let's begin," Olivia announces. The door bangs open and Dylan saunters in. "Just in time. Please find a mat."

"Did you tell him we'd be here?" I hiss at Indigo.

"Nope." She smirks. "It's serendipity."

It is not serendipity. There's nothing serendipitous about Dylan showing up at a yoga class I'm attending. It's stalking is what it is.

Dylan grins as he swaggers toward me. "You mind moving?" he asks the woman on my left. He points to me. "I want to be next to my friends."

"Sure," she breathes out. I roll my eyes. Slayed by Dylan's fake charm with one question.

"Good morning," he greets as he settles himself on the mat next to me.

I sniff and return my attention to the front of the room. I'll ignore him for the class. Dylan? Dylan who? I've found my new motto.

"If everyone is where they want to be," Olivia says and winks at Dylan. "We can begin."

"Sit in an easy pose in the center of your mat and allow your eyes to close. Begin to pay attention to the muscles in your face, relax your eyebrows, unclench your jaw, and soften your shoulders. Rid your body of tension and inhale a deep breath."

I try to pay attention as Olivia takes us through the breathing exercises. But how can I relax when with every breath I inhale, I smell Dylan's scent? It's clean and fresh. It reminds me of how laundry smells when you dry it outside in the spring. I want to wrap it around me before rolling in it.

I scowl at the thought and force myself to focus on what Olivia is saying. "Bring your arms up above your head and allow your palms to meet at the top, slowly bring them down in front of your sternum and rest in a seated Pranamasana."

"Seated what?" Dylan leans close to ask.

I glare at him until he leans back.

"Have you not had any coffee yet this morning?"

What part of my glare is he misunderstanding? This glare does not say 'speak to me'. It says, 'leave me the heck alone'.

"We'll grab some at the bakery on the way home."

"You're delusional," I hiss.

"I'll go for coffee with him," a woman in the row in front of us says.

"Sorry, darling. I'm a one woman man," Dylan says and she sighs.

"Let's stand and begin with the warrior pose," Olivia says before I can remind Dylan of how delusional he is.

"Left leg in front and bend your knee. Make sure your hips are turned forward and raise your arms in the air."

I follow the directions. This isn't bad. I thought yoga would be more difficult.

"Hold the pose. This asana will help strengthen your lower body, especially your hamstrings, glutes, and quadriceps," Olivia explains as she wanders through the room correcting people's poses.

She taps my hip. "Good job, bestie."

"What about me, teacher? How am I doing?" Dylan asks.

"Your hips should be forward facing. May I touch you?" At his nod, she places her hands on his hips and twists until they're turned toward the front. "There you go. Hold this pose."

She releases him to continue walking around the classroom.

"This doesn't feel natural," Dylan complains.

I notice his arms are trembling. My brow furrows. "Don't you have arm strength from playing the guitar?"

"I meant my legs."

Before I have a chance to respond, he wobbles to the side and tips over. I try to scooch out of the way but I'm not quick enough. He falls on me and we land on my mat in a mess of arms and legs.

"Shit. Virginia, are you okay? Did I hurt you?"

His hands run over my body checking for injuries. His fingers are calloused from playing the guitar. I've only ever been with men who have smooth hands before. But his calloused fingers roaming over my body feel better than anything I've felt with a smooth handed man before.

I should push him off of me. Any second now I'm going to push him off. Just as soon as I catch my breath. Considering his hands on me are causing me to lose my breath, it may be a while.

"You okay? Virginia?"

I realize I'm staring at his arms – his well-developed arms with hard muscles I wouldn't mind roaming my hands over – and lift my gaze to his face.

He blows out a breath. "Thank god. You're okay."

The relief on his face has me reeling. Does Dylan actually care for me? Am I more than a challenge to him?

He forgot he humiliated us, the voice in the back of my mind whispers. At the reminder, I reinforce my walls against a Dylan invasion.

Olivia kneels next to us. "I'm sorry, new bestie, but I think it's best if you and your boyfriend skip the rest of today's class."

"He's not my boyfriend."

"Not yet." She winks.

Dylan stands and offers me his hand. I accept it and he helps me to my feet.

"I guess we'll go have our coffee now."

His thumb rubs circles on my hand causing sparks to ignite throughout my body. I sway toward him until I remember. He doesn't know who I am.

I wrench my hand from his. "Sorry. I have someplace to be."

He sighs. I force myself to ignore how disappointed he sounds and leave the yoga studio before I give in to temptation.

Chapter 10

VIRGINIA

I stand with my hand on my doorknob. I need to go. I can't stay home when Indigo's having a birthday party. Even if Dylan's going to be there. She's my best friend. I can't not go.

I sniff. Do I feel a sinus infection coming on? Nope. My nostrils are clear. Dang it.

Fine. I'm going already.

I arrive at Indigo and Cash's house in less than five minutes. The house used to be Indigo's grandma's, but in a strange twist of events that proves life is crazier than fiction, Cash rented out the house at the exact same time as Indigo arrived to handle funeral arrangements for her grandma.

Now the high school sweethearts are madly in love again and living together. There have been hiccups along the way, but Cash fought for Indigo. I'm happy for my friend. She deserves a man who will do anything for her.

I stand on the porch studying their home. I could never afford this type of house. But it's my dream home.

I've always wanted a Colonial with a wraparound porch. I could read books on the porch swing every night. Preferably while my children run around the front yard. Little boys with blond hair and blue eyes who look like their father.

I force thoughts of Dylan out of my mind for the umpteenth time today and march to the front door. Since it's open, I don't bother knocking before I enter. The living room is packed with people, so I aim for the kitchen instead.

I enter the room and get an eyeful of Cash and Indigo going at it. He has her backed up against the refrigerator while he devours her mouth. It's sexier than any of my books. I whirl around to flee but in my haste hit the counter.

"Ouch." I rub my hip. Indigo and Cash pull apart. "Sorry. I was trying to give you some privacy but the counter jumped up and bit me."

Cash kisses Indigo's nose. "No worries. We'll finish this later."

"Hopefully when you're alone," I mutter and he barks out a laugh before squeezing my shoulder and walking out of the kitchen.

"Happy birthday!" I hand Indigo her gift.

"You didn't have to get me a present."

"Okay. I'll take it back then."

I make as if to grab the gift but she clutches it to her chest and angles away from me. "Mine. My precious."

"Open it." I bounce on my toes. She's going to love this.

She digs into the gift bag and removes three books. She gasps. "The entire Knockemout Series?"

"Open the first page."

She does and her eyes widen. "They're signed by Lucy Score!" She throws herself at me. "Thank you! This is awesome!"

"You're welcome."

She dances around the kitchen. I dance along with her since she won't release me. "Best birthday present ever."

"You can't expect me to do your taxes when you won't give me the receipts!" a woman shouts and we stop dancing.

"What's going on?" I ask.

Indigo grins. "Let's go find out."

We tiptoe out of the kitchen and into the living room where a woman and man are arguing with each other while everyone else stands in a circle around them as if arguing is a spectator sport.

"I gave you the receipts!" the man yells back.

"The man is Brody, one of Cash's step-brothers," Indigo whispers to me.

Cash and his brothers are another crazy story. When we knew him in high school, Cash was an only child *and* an orphan. But then he found his biological dad who had sadly already passed away but it turns out his bio dad had six other sons. All of whom live in Winter Falls.

"Who's the woman?"

"No idea."

Cash and the rest of the band join us. He slings an arm around Indigo. "It's Leia. She's Brody's new assistant."

Gibson cozies up to me. "How ya doing, Virginia?"

Dylan shoves him away. "No."

I glare at him. "What? I'm not good enough to be friends with the world famous band?"

"You're too good for the band and Gibson is a manwhore."

Gibson winks. "I prefer the term Cassanova."

"Do you know the original Cassanova was a librarian at the end of his life?"

Gibson's nose wrinkles. "Librarian?"

I try not to take offense at his obvious distaste for my profession and continue my lecture, "And his books are considered the most authentic sources of information about the customs and norms of European society during the 18th century."

Gibson pales. "Maybe Cassanova isn't my preferred term. Maybe I should use Lothario."

Before I can ruin his view of the word Lothario, Leia shouts again. "I don't know why I put up with you!"

"She appears a bit uptight." Gibson rubs his hands together in anticipation. "I think I know a way to relax her."

He starts toward Leia but Fender growls at him. "No."

"What no?"

"She's our neighbor."

"Too close for comfort." Gibson shivers and heads off in the direction opposite of where Leia and Brody are fighting.

"Poor Leia," a woman says as she takes Gibson's place next to me. "Brody is a trial to work with."

I smile at her. "I don't believe we've met."

She jostles the little girl in her arms. "I'm Soleil."

"And you work with Brody?"

She groans. "Oh, dear lord, no. I live with him." She smiles at her baby. "And this is his daughter."

Before I have a chance to ask her what she means, she forces her way in between Leia and Brody. They speak together in low tones before Leia stomps off.

Indigo claps her hands. "Show's over, folks!"

I eye the door. I've had enough drama and definitely enough peopling for one day, but Indigo grasps my wrist to stop me.

"You just got here," she pouts. She sticks out her bottom lip and everything.

"Thirty-year-olds aren't supposed to pout."

"I won't if you stay." I hesitate. "At least for one drink."

"What kind of drinks do you have?"

"I happen to have connections with the *Naked Falls Brewery* and I may have a batch of their latest IPA." She grins because she knows she has me now. I'm addicted to IPAs but their higher cost means I don't drink them as often as I'd like.

"You're manipulative."

"And you're a sore loser."

When it comes to not getting what I want, I don't enjoy losing. Huh. I guess I am a sore loser.

We grab two bottles from the refrigerator before wandering outside where most of the guests are gathered. Cash is grilling, and his bandmates are gathered around him.

I order my eyes to look away, but they don't listen. Not when there's a perfect specimen of man in my view. Since it's a warm day, Dylan has ditched his jeans for a pair of shorts. His legs should be pasty white considering it's spring. But no, he already sports a tan.

And those thighs? They're annoyingly perfect. Not too muscular so he resembles a bodybuilder. And not too skinny either. Exactly the right size to hold onto while I kneel in front of him.

I wave a hand in front of my face as it heats while images of all the things I could do to Dylan flit through my mind.

Indigo nudges me. "You should tell him what happened."

"Tell who what?"

She snorts. "You're funny."

"I'm ready for the meat," Cash hollers at her.

"Hold my beer." She hands me her bottle before going inside.

"How are you, Virginia?"

I groan. I'm an idiot. I should have helped Indigo instead of standing here all alone. Making myself the perfect target for Dylan and his lame come-ons.

"I'm on my way home."

He raises an eyebrow at my nearly full beer but I ignore him.

"Can you hold Indigo's beer?"

He accepts the beer, but he doesn't leave me alone. I should be so lucky. He sets the bottle on the nearest surface and motions to the door.

"Come on. I'll walk you home."

I roll my eyes. "I don't need you to walk me home. I'm perfectly capable of walking myself home."

"Nonetheless. It would be my honor."

I snort. "Your honor? Bologna."

His brow wrinkles. "What do you mean? Bologna."

"Isn't it obvious? You only want to go with me so you can hit on me again."

"Hey now. I've never hit on you."

I raise my eyebrows. "Really? That's the story you're going with."

"It's true. I admit I've asked you out, but I've never hit on you."

"Fine!" I throw my hands in the air and end up spilling beer down my shirt.

"Let me get you a napkin."

"Can you stop? Just stop."

He freezes. "Stop what?"

I make a circle with my finger. "Whatever this is. Being nice to me. Pretending you want to date me. Enough."

"I'm not pretending. I do want to date you."

Ugh! He infuriates me! "You don't know me."

"Thus, the date."

"Which is why you wanted to date me before."

"Before? What do you mean before?"

Gosh dang it. Why did I mention before?

His brow wrinkles as he studies my face. "Do we know each other from somewhere?"

I might as well tell him. I won't be able to keep my humiliation a secret forever. No matter how much I want to dig a hole in Indigo's yard to hide myself in. It's impossible. My upper body muscle strength is non-existent and I don't own a shovel.

I set my beer down on the nearest table and cross my arms over my chest. "Yes, we know each other from somewhere."

Dylan scratches his chin. "From where?"

"From high school," I admit.

"I don't remember you."

"No kidding," I huff.

"How can I not remember you? Were you in a different year than me?"

Is he serious? "You are some piece of work."

"Okay. We were in the same year. Did we have any classes together?"

I shake my head. He is serious.

He smiles. "There you have it. We didn't have any classes together. That's why I don't remember you."

"Except I was friends with Indigo."

The smile falls from his face. I might as well strike while the iron's hot.

"And I asked you to the Sadie Hawkin's dance."

He grimaces.

"Do you know what you said?"

His cheeks flame and he ducks his head. "No."

I poke his chest. "You said. And I quote here. Sorry, I can't. And then walked away without another word."

"I can explain."

"Save your explanations. I don't need them."

This time when I try to leave, he doesn't stop me. Good. It's over. Him chasing after me, asking me out, showing up wherever I am, is over.

I should be happy. Except my heart feels as if it's being torn in two. Stupid heart.

Chapter 11

DYLAN

I stare at the destruction of my apartment. I've searched everywhere I can think of but no high school yearbook. What am I doing? I wouldn't have my yearbook with me. This isn't my home. My home is in San Diego. For now, at least.

I dig out my phone and dial Mom.

"Hey, favorite son of mine."

I roll my eyes. "I'm your only son, Mom."

"Thus, my favorite."

"You're a nut."

"How are you, my boy?"

I open my mouth to ask if she knows where my yearbook from senior year is but she continues before I have the chance.

"Any news? Do you have a girlfriend? I can't wait forever to become a grandma."

"Mom, you already are a grandma. Did you forget Janis has two boys?"

"But I want you to have a wife and children."

"And I will."

"You will? Did you meet someone?"

I chuckle. "I meant in the future." In the near future, if I have my way. But I need to fix my fuck up first.

"You're not the youngest anymore."

"Mom, I'm twenty-nine. I have time."

She sighs. "What else have you been up to?"

I fill her in on the album we're recording and how it's going. And then we chat for a few minutes about my sisters before I hang up.

Damn. How am I going to figure out who Virginia is now? I can't ask Mom for my yearbook. She'd ferret out I have 'girl' issues and be on the next plane to Denver to meet her. But I don't have a girlfriend. Unlike Cash who has the love of his life in his arms right now.

Hold on. Indigo and Virginia were friends in high school. She's bound to have the yearbook. If not, she can fill me in on all the details. I send Cash a message and ask him to come over ASAP.

I'm nearly finished picking up the mess I made of my apartment when Cash bursts inside. "What's the emergency?"

"What happened?" Gibson asks as enters with Jett and Gibson.

I groan. "You had to bring the entire band with you?"

"And me!" Indigo is the last to arrive.

Cash shrugs. "I can't help it. They stick to me like barnacles."

"Ew." Gibson makes a face. "Gross. I'm not a barnacle. I'm a cute and cuddly koala."

Indigo laughs. "Do you know half of the wildlife population of koalas has chlamydia?"

"I do not have chlamydia. I get tested regularly." Gibson sounds proud of himself.

"Maybe you should stop comparing yourself to animals and people, Casanova." I make sure to emphasize the Casanova.

"Librarian." Gibson shivers.

"What's wrong with a librarian?"

"Nothing when the librarian is a sexy thing like yours is."

He's lucky I don't hit him. But I won't since he recognized how Virginia is mine. And she will be – as soon as she realizes I'm not an asshole.

"Ten bucks says the 'emergency' has to do with Virginia," Jett says.

Gibson rolls his eyes. "No bet. Of course, it has to do with Virginia."

Fender grunts in agreement before making a beeline for the kitchen and opening the refrigerator. "There's no food in here."

"Is there food in your refrigerator?"

"Yes."

"Big guy here keeps us fully stocked," Jett says.

Fender glares at him. "Stop eating my food."

Jett bats his eyelashes. "What happened to what's mine is yours?"

"What's mine is mine."

Cash whistles. "Let's solve Dylan's problem and then we'll go to the brewery for some food."

Gibson bursts into laughter. "We can't solve Dylan's problem in a day. He needs to grovel for at least a year before Virginia will deign to speak to him."

I scowl. "What do you know about it?"

Indigo raises her hand. "I told him. In my defense, they threatened to storm over here if I didn't."

I snort. "Good thing you kept them from storming over here."

She grimaces. "Oops."

"Dude." Jett shakes his head. "I can't believe you turned down Virginia the way you did. Cold."

"Not all of us can be charming." Gibson winks.

"I don't remember. I don't remember her asking me out," I admit. To my utter shame, I don't remember Virginia at all.

"How can you not remember a girl asking you out? You're not me," Gibson says, and I reassess my decision not to hit him.

I crack my knuckles as I study where I should punch him first.

"No," Cash growls.

"No what?"

"No, you're not going to hit Gibson. You're the peacemaker, not the fighter."

"Why can't I be both?" Cash raises his eyebrows and I sigh. "Fine, I can't be both."

"How are we going to fix this?" Indigo asks and brings us back to the matter at hand. Mainly, how big of an asshole I am.

"Was I an asshole in high school?"

Indigo flinches. Shit. There's my answer. I was. I bury my face in my hands. I guess I can say goodbye to any future with Virginia. She's never going to forgive me. And I can't blame her if I was an asshole.

"Dylan," Cash says and I drop my hands. "You were working two jobs, going to high school, and playing in a band. You were overwhelmed."

"Pretty sure none of those excuse me for being an asshole. Mom would be appalled if she knew." I should send her some flowers for having to put up with me.

"You weren't an asshole," Indigo claims.

"Which is why you flinched when I asked you before."

"You weren't an asshole all the time." She pauses. "But the way you shot Virginia down when she asked you out? Bit of an asshole move."

"I need to remember. Maybe if I remember, I'll figure out why I was such an asshole to her."

Indigo plops the yearbook down on the coffee table. "I brought this but I don't know if it'll help."

I snatch the book up. "Sadie Hawkins," I mumble as I flip through the pictures until I find a two-page spread of the dance.

"What is Sadie Hawkins anyway?" Jett asks.

"It's a turnabout dance. The girls ask the boys instead of the usual way around," Indigo explains.

"I prefer to do the asking myself," Gibson says.

Indigo ignores him. "It's usually held in November."

I freeze. "Did you say November?"

"Yeah." She leans forward and taps the page. "The date's right here."

I close the book and hand it to her. "No wonder I don't remember," I say but don't explain further.

"Okay, I'll bite. Why don't you remember?" Jet asks.

"November our senior year of high school was the coldest November in decades." I pause. I hate admitting how I failed my family back then. These guys know everything about me, but still. It hurts to remember how I wasn't there for my family.

"It's not your fault," Cash growls.

"No? Whose fault was it? It certainly wasn't Mom's or Janis' or Joni's or Linda's or Stevie's!"

Indigo holds up a hand. "I know you're having a moment here but is everyone in your family named after a musician?"

"Indy," Cash admonishes.

"What? It can't be a coincidence."

I run a hand through my hair. "It's not. My dad loved rock. And my mom indulged him. She indulged him way too much."

She put up with his various affairs because she loved him and he said they were meaningless. Until the day he took off with his secretary and left us behind. She never heard from him again. She had to divorce the asshole in absentia.

"Okay. Back to November. What happened to make you into a martyr?" Indigo asks.

I glare at her, and Cash growls at me in warning. I drop the glare and blow out a breath of air.

"I didn't pay the gas bill. We had no heat."

"Indy's right. There's no reason to make yourself a martyr about this. You were just a kid."

I slam a fist against my chest. "I was the man in the family. I was responsible."

"As much as I'm enjoying watching Dylan beat himself up," Jett says and I snap my teeth at him. "Shouldn't we be coming up with some plan of action for him to get his girl back?"

"Virginia isn't my girl."

"Not with that attitude she isn't."

"There's an easy solution."

I cock my eyebrow at Gibson. What could possibly be easy about this situation?

"Tell Virginia the truth." He stands. "Now, who's ready for some food?"

Fender grunts. "He's right."

Jett and Cash nod in agreement.

"What do you think, Indigo?"

I'm not accepting my bandmates' opinions without hearing from a woman on the matter.

"I think Virginia will forgive you if you tell her the truth."

Hope sparks in my chest. "I have a chance?"

"You have a chance."

The spark of hope grows as I follow my bandmates and Indigo out the door. It won't be easy to reveal the truth to Virginia, but I'll do it. Anything to get her to forgive me for being an asshole to her.

Chapter 12

VIRGINIA

I frown at Dylan through the peephole. I didn't think I'd see him again after I told him I'm the mouse he doesn't remember from high school.

"I have meatloaf and potatoes from the diner."

My stomach growls loud enough for him to hear through the door. I love meatloaf and potatoes. Especially if someone else cooked them.

When I don't respond, he sighs. "I'll leave the food in front of the door."

Virginia Hale, be nice!

I promise I'm not usually a mean girl. But when Dylan's around all I can think about is how I was the forgettable mouse in high school, and I become someone I'm not proud of. But enough is enough.

I open the door. "Please, come in."

He smiles and his dimple makes an appearance. I have to clutch the doorknob before I raise my hand to trace the indent with my finger.

He lifts the food in the air. "I thought we could eat together."

I bite my bottom lip as I consider his offer.

He moans. "I want to pull your bottom lip from your teeth. With my teeth."

I gasp. He does? "But I'm the mouse."

He scowls. "You're not a mouse."

"Yeah, right. Which is why you remembered me from high school."

"Crap. I need to explain."

"Explain why you were a complete jerk when I finally managed to gather the courage to ask you out? Explain why you humiliated me?" I snort. "Sure. Let's hear it."

"Can we eat first?"

I accept the plates from him and set them on the dining table. "Explanation first. Food second."

I wish I was Indigo. She'd have thrown the food at him and slammed the door in his face. But I'm not. I'm Virginia the mouse.

I've worked hard to rid myself of my mouse tendencies. But they always come back. Usually when I need them to stay away the most.

"My dad walked out on my family when I was a sophomore in high school."

I fist my hands to stop myself from hugging him. "I'm sorry."

He waves away my sympathy. "It wasn't a big loss. He wasn't much of a father." He blows out a puff of air. "But when he took off, he *took off*. He emptied the bank accounts, packed up his shit, and rode off into the sunset with his secretary. Mom never heard from him again."

My mouth gapes open. "You never heard from again?"

"Mom searched for him. She needed the money. She had five kids at home to feed and clothe and was a stay at home mom. Dad didn't want her working. He said it made him look bad."

His wife working reflected poorly on him? What a jerk.

"Mom never did find him. She divorced him in absentia."

"But you're his children? Didn't he ever contact you?"

"Once." He runs a hand through his hair. "We were on tour after our first album took off. He showed up backstage at our concert in LA. He barely greeted me before asking for money." He growls. "As if I would give money to the asshole who left my mom to fend for five kids on her own."

I grasp his hand and pull him down on the sofa. "Did you tell your mom about his visit?"

He shakes his head. "Tell her the man she still loves lives less than two hours away? No way."

"Your mom still loves him?"

He frowns. "She fell apart when he left. She couldn't believe he left her for another woman. Don't get me wrong. It wasn't a surprise he wanted another woman. He wasn't faithful. He paraded his infidelity in front of her and she allowed it. She thought if she didn't yell or threaten him, he'd stay."

"I'm sorry," I murmur.

I hesitate. His story is sad and I feel bad for what he had to endure, but why is he confessing this to me now?

"You're wondering why I'm telling you my pathetic story."

"You're not pathetic." I bump his shoulder. "But I am curious why you're telling me your story now."

"I'm trying to explain why I was an asshole to you in high school."

"You were going through a lot. I understand."

He grasps my chin. "Don't do that."

"Do what?" How can I possibly remember what when he's touching me? When his calloused fingers are caressing my cheek? Making my body tremble and warmth spread throughout me?

"Don't let me off the hook."

"Don't you want me to let you off the hook?"

"I do."

His eyes heat and a shiver runs through my body. I want to drown in his warmth. He leans down and I sway toward him. My gaze drops to his mouth. What will his lips feel like on mine? Will they be soft? Will they be hard?

Is he a good kisser? I bet he is. After all, he's had tons of practice.

Good reminder. Dylan isn't merely some old friend from high school. He's a rockstar. A rockstar who would never be interested in me. The mouse.

I clear my throat and pull away.

He drops his hand from my chin. "Sorry."

"You were saying…"

I have no idea what he was saying. What were we discussing again? Why didn't I let him kiss me?

"When Dad left, I got a job – two actually – to help Mom pay the bills. It was hard for Mom to secure a good-paying job since she had no prior experience. Plus, she had my sisters to care for. I took over as much as I could – driving Stevie, Linda, and Joni to school and their after-school activities."

"Hold on. You had two jobs and helped care for your sisters while you were in high school?" He nods. "How did I not know this?"

His cheeks darken. "Nobody did. Except Cash. I didn't want anyone to feel sorry for me."

"Feel sorry for you? Not a chance. You're amazing."

He ignores my compliment. "I barely remember high school. It's a blur of working late nights, studying for tests, and dealing with my sisters. The only good part was the band. I didn't remember you asked me out until Indigo told me the dance was in November."

"What was in November?"

He frowns. "I fucked up. I didn't pay the gas bill. I thought I could skip a month and it would be okay. But it wasn't. The gas company shut us off. My sisters were all frantic because they couldn't shower."

"The message," I mutter.

"What?"

Gah! This is so embarrassing. "After I…" My face heats but I plow forward. "Asked you out. You got a message and rushed off. I thought you were running away from me…"

He tucks a strand of hair behind my ear. "I would never run away from you."

"But you never noticed me either." The words are out before I can stop them. "Ignore me. I shouldn't have spoken. You didn't have the time to notice me."

"Nonetheless, I can't believe I didn't notice you."

I roll my eyes. "No need to flatter me. You're forgiven for humiliating me in high school."

How can I not forgive him? I know how it feels to have demons in high school. To keep your head down to avoid being noticed.

"Thank you. I'm not sure I deserve your forgiveness but I'll take it. And I am truly sorry I humiliated you. I would beat the shit out of any guy who humiliated my sisters the way I did you."

I raise my eyebrows. Dylan doesn't seem to be the violent type. "Do you usually go around beating up your sisters' boyfriends?"

"No, but I might have threatened a few of them. Well, me and my bandmates. Fender is especially handy in these situations. He doesn't need to speak a word and the assholes run away from my sisters."

"Were you always this protective of your sisters?"

Stop talking, Virginia! I don't need to know Dylan is the protector type. It's bad enough my body longs for him. I can't get my heart involved.

"Even before Dad left, he wasn't around much. Working full-time and carrying on multiple affairs is time consuming. Someone had to step up and be the man of the house."

"Must be nice to have someone in your corner," I mumble.

He brushes a hand over my cheek. "If you let me, I'll be in your corner."

I'm tempted. More than tempted. I've never had a protector before. I've always had to look after myself. My mom certainly didn't protect me the way she should have.

But this isn't Dylan from high school. The cute boy with his mop of hair always falling in his eyes. This is Dylan Mitchell. Lead guitar player for *Cash & the Sinners,* a world-famous band.

"What do you say, Virginia? Will you go out on a date with me?"

I love how he doesn't play games. He comes right out and says what he wants. And he's nice about it. No demanding. No telling me I'm lucky he would date me.

But what happens when he leaves Winter Falls? He doesn't live in town. He's only here to record an album. Once it's finished, he'll be off back to San Diego. And I am not living in San Diego again. Never ever.

"I don't think it's a good idea," I finally say.

"It's not a good idea. It's an excellent idea."

I roll my eyes. "Let's stick to being friends."

"I'm a great friend. I bring you food." His stomach rumbles and I giggle.

"Let's eat."

He stands and holds out his hand. I grab it and he helps me to my feet. "I'm not giving up on you, Virginia."

"Friends," I remind him.

"You can't resist me forever."

I don't need to resist him forever. He'll be gone from Winter Falls soon enough. I rub a hand over my stomach when it protests Dylan's absence. Better to miss a friend than end up brokenhearted.

Chapter 13

Forgiveness – easier to ask for than permission

Dylan

I set my guitar on its stand. "Are we done for the day?"

It's still early. But we've already finished recording one song and I'm ready to get out of here. I want to install the gifts I bought for Virginia before she returns home from work. It'll be a surprise to her, but better to ask for forgiveness than permission.

"Why? Do you have someplace to be?" Jett asks.

"Twenty bucks says wherever he has to be, has something to do with Virginia," Gibson says.

"But she continues to shoot him down." Jett taps out the intro to *Loser*.

I throw my pick at him. "I am not a loser."

Cash chuckles and I glare at him. "As much shit as you've given me about Indy over the past years, you can't complain now."

"I could give you some lessons in how to charm a woman," Gibson offers.

I cross my arms over my chest. "I do not need charm lessons from a manwhore."

Gibson sighs. "I've explained this. I'm not a whore if I don't get paid."

Fender grunts.

Gibson wags a finger at him. "No lip from you."

"My bedroom is next to yours," Fender grumbles. "I should get hazardous duty pay."

"Jett's the one who enjoys hazards. Not me."

Fender cocks his eyebrow. "And you didn't have a naked woman scratching the hell out of you because you kicked her out of your bed last night."

Gibson smirks. "She was wild."

"And you were drunk and weaving all over the place while she went at you. Guess who picked up the glass she broke and escorted her out of the house when your drunk ass passed out?"

"It wasn't me," Jett pipes in.

I share a look with Cash. Do we need to worry about Gibson's drinking? He's always been a big drinker. But passing out on a normal weeknight? This is concerning.

"No," Gibson growls. "No interventions. No bullshit about my drinking. I've got it under control."

I doubt it but he's not ready to tackle his problem. And if he's not ready? It's not worth our time and energy.

"Whatever, man," I say. "Your life. Your choice. I'm out of here."

I hurry out of the studio before anyone can stop me. I love my bandmates but they can be supreme assholes sometimes –

especially when they know the woman I want isn't giving me the time of day.

Once at my apartment, I grab the security cameras and new locks. I'll install the security cameras first since I don't need to get inside Virginia's apartment to do the work.

The front door camera is easy. I have it mounted in no time. The camera for her balcony door is a bit more difficult. I need to get onto her balcony to install it.

I could get a ladder and climb up onto the balcony, but I don't want everyone in town to know what I'm up to. And, rest assured, the people of Winter Falls would be out in force if they saw me climbing a ladder onto Virginia's balcony. One thing I've learned in the short time I've been here is how nosey everyone in town is.

Instead, I knock on the neighbor's door and ask if I can use their balcony. It's an easy climb from their balcony onto Virginia's. Too easy. Any intruder could manage it without any special equipment. Good thing I'm installing this camera.

The balcony door flies open. "What are you doing?" Virginia shouts.

I motion toward the packaging on her bistro table. "Isn't it obvious?"

"Obvious?" She rears back. "What is obvious about you invading my house without my permission?"

"I didn't invade your house. I specifically didn't install the new locks because I knew you wouldn't want me in your house without you being there."

"New locks?"

I lift the new lock I bought her. "New lock."

She blows out a breath. "I have no idea what's happening here."

"I'm installing security cameras and new locks in your apartment."

"But why?" She pauses. "Did something happen? Did someone break into my house? Is Harry okay?"

She spins around and rushes off to her bedroom. I follow. She lifts the blanket off of a cage on her dresser. Her hedgehog snuffles and she opens the cage to cuddle him.

"Hello, my sweet Harry," she coos to him as she pets him.

I want her to pet me the way she's petting him. To skim her hands all over my body. My cock perks up at the idea. Shit. I'm jealous of a hedgehog.

"No one broke into your house."

Her shoulders relax. "Good. But why are you putting in all these security measures if no one broke in? Isn't Winter Falls supposed to be safe?"

"There's a difference between being safe and feeling safe."

"Explain."

Crap. This is not going as I expected. I thought she'd come home and be pleasantly surprised with my efforts. Maybe throw herself at me in gratitude.

Damn. I'm an asshole. I shouldn't be adding security to her apartment for my own gain.

I clear my throat. "Stevie, my youngest sister, had nightmares after Dad left."

"That sucks," she says as we settle on the couch.

"She'd wake up screaming certain someone was in the house." Her screams were terrifying. And Mom wasn't there. She was usually working third shift so she could be home in the evenings as much as possible.

"No matter what I said or what I did, Stevie was terrified. I explained how safe the house was. How the doors and windows were shut and locked. How low the crime rate in the neighborhood was. Nothing helped. Until I installed a security system. The system made her feel safe when I couldn't."

She grasps my hand. "You didn't fail her."

I frown. "I did fail her. I couldn't make her feel safe."

She squeezes my hand. "Silly man. You made her feel safe when you installed the security system. You did that."

Maybe. I'm not sure. I am sure I don't want to discuss my childhood with Virginia. No need to remind her of what an asshole I was.

"Anyway, I thought installing cameras and locks would make you feel safe."

She releases my hand. I miss her soft hand in mine. I would love to feel those soft fingers roving all over my body. I bet her touch would be tentative at first. But Virginia is no mouse. A few words from me and she'd be certain of her right to touch me. To make me feel good.

My cock begins to harden and I shut those thoughts down. I'm here to make Virginia feel safe. Not to maul her.

"Why do you think I don't feel safe?"

I shrug. I don't want to mention how her face softened when I offered to walk her home from *Electric Vibes.* Or how her claim that she doesn't need me to make her feel safe set off warning bells in my mind.

"Indigo mentioned this is the first time you've ever lived alone. And I remembered how I installed cameras and extra locks for Stevie when she moved into her first apartment last year."

"You're still looking after your sisters?"

"Someone has to. They're a bunch of troublemakers otherwise."

"And you have four sisters?"

I nod. "Janis, Joni, Linda, and Stevie."

Her brow furrows. "And you're Dylan."

I waggle my eyebrows. "At your service."

"Are all of you named after rockstars?"

"Yep. Janis Joplin, Joni Mitchell, Linda Ronstadt, and Stevie Nicks, although Joni Mitchell is more of a folksinger than rockstar. My asshole dad had a thing for rockers and my mom indulged him."

"And they're all troublemakers?"

"Ask me about the time they showed up at one of our concerts demanding entrance backstage claiming I'd stolen all of their songs and lyrics. I don't even write the lyrics for the band. Cash does. But they created a huge ruckus. The local news did a feature on how *Cash & the Sinners* were a bunch of hacks stealing songs from four poor sisters."

"You wouldn't give them backstage passes?"

I groan. "My sisters and my mom can always get backstage. All of our security knows who they are. All they have to do is show up and they're in."

She giggles. "But they created a ruckus instead."

"Told you. Troublemakers."

My sisters can be the biggest troublemakers in the world if it makes Virginia giggle. She's adorable when she laughs. Her nose scrunches up and she makes these little snorts. Adorable.

"What did your mom say?"

"She's used to their antics by now. As long as they ring her every Sunday and show up for dinner once a month and on the holidays, she doesn't bother."

"Do you talk to your mom every Sunday?"

I narrow my eyes on her. "Are you saying I'm a mama's boy?"

She shrugs. "If the pacifier fits."

"Oh, and now I'm a baby?" She giggles again and lightness fills me. She's innocent and pure and everything I want. "You're lucky you're holding Harry."

She cocks her head to the side. "Why's that?"

"Otherwise, I'd tickle you to punish you."

"Maybe I'm not ticklish." The blush on her cheeks tells a different story.

I can't wait to prove her wrong but first I have a job to finish. I stand. "Shall I finish installing the camera on your balcony?"

She bites her lip as she studies me. I'd stand here all day to let her get her fill. Except my cock enjoys the idea entirely too much and begins to harden. I clear my throat.

"The camera?"

"Yes, please."

Her softly spoken please is not helping calm my cock down. Not at all. He wants her to whisper please while she's naked beneath me.

"I'll er…"

I hurry away before Virginia notices how much I want her. And I do want her. She's perfect for me. Soft and sweet and full of light but she's no pushover. My little librarian has a backbone of steel.

Chapter 14

Bells – not appropriate in a library but apparently movies are

VIRGINIA

"Movie night is tonight," Gratitude says as she opens the door to exit the library for the day. "Make sure everything is put back exactly as it was."

"Movie night?" I call before she can leave.

"All the information you need is in a folder marked movie night." And then she's gone before I can ask any more questions.

What in the world? Why is this the first I'm hearing about movie night? I was planning an early night with a bubble bath and a new book from Pippa Grant.

I locate the 'movie night' folder at the circulation desk and open it. I gasp at the floor plan. I'm supposed to move all the tables and chairs around? Thanks, Gratitude. You couldn't have stayed and helped?

There's only one thing to do.

"Hey, Virginia," Indigo answers.

"Are you busy?" I plow on before she can answer. "I kind of need some help."

"No problem. Where are you?"

"The library."

"On my way with bells on."

She hangs up before I can remind her bells in a library aren't a good idea. Although, there's also movie night at the library so maybe I have no idea what I'm talking about.

The library door opens not two minutes later.

"You were quick," I say as I turn around to discover it's not Indigo but Dylan and the band.

"We were at the studio when Indigo phoned to say you needed help," Dylan says.

He smiles and his adorable dimple makes an appearance. A dimple I'm finding hard to resist since I learned why he humiliated me in high school. As far as excuses go, his is probably the best I've heard and I'm a librarian who's heard every excuse there can possibly be for why a book was returned late.

Gibson flexes his bicep. "I'm the muscle."

Fender grunts before shoving him.

"Hey! It's not 'treat Gibson like a punching bag' day!" Gibson protests as he hits the wall.

"It's not? Sounds like fun. When is it my turn?" Jett asks.

Cash forces his way between Jett and Gibson. "Enough."

"We're here to help Ginny. Not create more work for her," Dylan grumbles.

Ginny? Who's Ginny? Does he mean me?

"What do you want us to do?" Cash asks and draws me out of my contemplation of why a nickname makes butterflies in my stomach explode.

I hold up the floor plan. "We need to move a bunch of furniture to set up for movie night."

"Movie night?" Jett perks up. "There's a movie night in Winter Falls?"

"Not if you don't help me get the furniture rearranged."

"Oh, the librarian's feisty. Me likey." Gibson waggles his eyebrows.

I try to scowl at him, but he's beyond ridiculous and I end up giggling.

Dylan snags the floor plan from my hand. "Come on. Let's get the furniture moved before you numbskulls find another distraction."

"Who you calling a numbskull?" Jett asks.

Gibson elbows him. "Obviously you."

Dylan sighs. "I apologize for them, Ginny. They followed me over here. I couldn't get rid of them."

That's the second time he called me Ginny. "What's with the nickname?"

His cheeks darken. Oh my gosh. Is he embarrassed? How adorable!

"I thought the name Ginny suited you. Do you hate it?"

Hate it? Why would I hate the man I'm obsessed with – despite my best intentions to ignore him – giving me a nickname?

"Considering the original Virginia was a Roman girl who was killed by her father in order to save her from seduction by a corrupt government official, I'm okay with it."

His eyes widen. "Her father killed her? Ginny it is then."

"What's Ginny?" Gibson asks.

Dylan pushes him away. "None of your business."

"You're silly." Gibson chuckles. "Everything's my business."

Cash clears his throat. "All right, numbskulls. Let's get to work."

Jett points to Gibson. "He means you."

"Work," Fender grunts.

Cash starts ordering everyone around and I let him. I might not be the scared mouse I once was in high school, but I'm still a shy introvert who prefers to hang back and observe while someone else is in charge.

Fender picks up one side of a table and I hurry to help him. He grunts at me.

"Sorry, big buy. I don't speak grunt."

"I got this."

I roll my eyes. "Yeah, yeah. You're all big and manly with a boatload of testosterone. We're all duly impressed. Can we move the table now?"

He smiles and his face goes from King of the Grumps to bad boy hot guy. Whoa!

Dylan nudges me out of the way. "I'll help him."

I fist my hands on my hips. "I never pegged you for a male chauvinist pig."

"Not a chauvinist pig. But I do want to show off my muscles for you."

He flexes his biceps and I have to admit they are pretty impressive. Especially the arm with the tattoo. I was jealous of those girls' names inked on his arm before but my jealousy vanished when I realized those names are his sisters'.

"Fine. You're not a chauvinist pig. You're a pretty boy."

He gasps. "Pretty boy? I am not a pretty boy."

"If the veneers fit."

"I am not some vain Hollywood actor with veneers."

"Especially not after he lost his front tooth in that bar fight," Cash hollers.

"Bar fight? You were in a bar fight?"

"It was Cash's fault." Dylan leans close to whisper-shout. "It's why his nose isn't perfect anymore."

"Indy says the bump on my nose makes me appear distinguished."

Dylan snorts. "Because she's love blind."

"You're just jealous because you've never been voted *Time*'s sexiest man alive."

"Neither have you."

"Is this how they act all the time?" I ask Fender. He grunts in response. "I'll assume your grunt is a yes." He winks.

"Fender," Dylan growls at him. "No."

No what? No grunting. He grunts all the time. Hold on. Does he mean the wink? Is he angry at Fender for winking at me? Is he jealous?

I should probably be annoyed at the idea of him being jealous. But I'm not. Someone wants me? And doesn't want anyone else to have me? It makes me feel all warm and fuzzy inside.

Fender barks out a laugh. "Too easy," he says and begins carrying the table away.

Since Dylan's holding the other side of the table, he's forced to help Fender. As they move the table to a different area, my eyes are glued to Dylan's ass moving in his jeans. I've always had a thing for men in faded jeans. Although, I have a thing for everything Dylan related.

Enough obsessing over the rockstar. I scan the room to figure out how I can help. The men are moving the tables. I guess I can do the chairs.

I pick up the closest chair and start to carry it to where they're stacking the tables. Dylan snags it from me. "Thanks," he says with a wink.

I sigh before returning for another chair. This one he steals from me before I manage to lift it.

I throw my arms in the air. "What am I supposed to do?"

"Beer run!" Gibson shouts.

Dylan frowns. "No beer but some coffee would be nice."

"And maybe some of those amazing chocolate cupcakes from *Bake Me Happy*," Jett adds.

"Here." Dylan sets the chair down and digs out his wallet.

I place a hand on his wrist to stop him. "I got it."

"Okay," he gives in.

"Five black coffees and five chocolate cupcakes coming up."

"Thanks, Ginny." Dylan smiles and out comes the dimple. I swear he knows his dimple makes me weak in the knees and is wielding it to break my defenses. I'm afraid it's working.

It takes me less than five minutes to arrive at *Bake Me Happy* since the bakery is kitty-corner across the square from the library.

"Here you go." Bryan, the bakery worker, offers me a tray with mugs of coffee and the cupcakes.

"How did you know?"

"Your man phoned in your order. He is one delicious specimen." He sighs. "One of these days a rockstar is going to come to Winter Falls and play for my team."

He nudges the tray toward me but I hold up a hand to stop him. "He's not my man and I need to pay."

"No need to pay. Your man already did."

I scowl. "He tricked me. We agreed I'd pay."

"I'd let him pay for whatever he wants to pay for if I were you."

"Easier said than done," I mumble as I accept the tray from him.

"Enjoy the ride, honey bear. Enjoy the ride," he says as he opens the door for me.

I blow him a kiss before crossing the street to the library. When I enter, I don't see the guys and go in search of them.

"Ginny? You call Virginia Ginny now?" Cash asks and I stop to eavesdrop.

"She prefers it," Dylan says. I do. It gives me tingles every time he says Ginny instead of Virginia.

"She prefers it," Gibson mimics. "What else does she prefer?"

"Knock it off. Ginny is a lady and you will treat her as such," Dylan grumbles and my insides quiver.

I want to hear his low growly voice while he's kissing me and touching me. Exploring every inch of me. I start to fan my face before I remember I'm holding a drinks tray. I blow out a breath and order my hormones to calm down.

"The question is do you treat her like a lady?" Jett asks.

"I don't kiss and tell."

"But you have kissed? How was it? I bet underneath her uptight librarian exterior she's hiding a tiger," Gibson says.

"I told you. I don't kiss and tell."

"Dylan and Virginia sitting in a tree. K–I–S–S–I–N–G," Jett sings.

"Tease me all you want. I don't care. She's worth it."

At Dylan's declaration, hope flares inside me. Maybe I can date a rockstar? Maybe I am worthy? Maybe I can give a date with him a try?

Chapter 15

DYLAN

I whistle as I climb the steps to the library. Today is a good day. The band worked on a new song, and I get to see Virginia twice.

Two encounters equals two chances to chip away at her walls. I know better than to try and bust her walls down. Ginny is a woman you have to finesse, not conquer.

"He's here!" a woman shouts the second I enter.

Damn. I thought tonight was a Winter Falls affair without tourists. I don't want to deal with screaming fans when I'm trying to convince an extremely skittish librarian to give me a chance.

The woman rolls her eyes. "Stop making a face. I don't care if you're a famous rockstar. I'm married to a movie star."

"What?"

"I'm Juniper." She sticks out her hand.

"Dylan."

"I'm in charge of the movie night."

I raise an eyebrow. "In charge? I didn't notice you here when we were re-arranging the furniture."

"The guys re-arrange the furniture."

I cross my arms over my chest. "I think you mean. Thank you, Dylan, for moving all the tables and chairs."

She giggles. "The gossip gals are at it again."

"Explain yourself."

"Enjoy the ride, Dylan, lead guitar player for *Cash & the Sinners*. Enjoy the ride."

Jett claps me on the back. "What ride are we taking?"

Juniper wags a finger at him. "It's not your turn."

He rocks back on his heels. "I can wait."

"You're going to be a fun one."

He winks. "I am fun."

A man who resembles Maverick Langston throws an arm around her shoulders. "You'll be having fun with someone else."

Jett's jaw drops open. "Are you Maverick Langston?"

"Are you Jett from *Cash & the Sinners*?"

Jett shakes his head. "Sorry. I didn't expect to meet an actor in Winter Falls."

"You never know what's going to happen in Winter Falls."

I know what I want to happen. I want my little librarian to fall for me. Where is Ginny anyway? I scan the room and spot her on the other side chatting with Indigo.

"Excuse me." I don't bother to wait for their replies and stalk across the room toward the object of my obsession.

Since we left the library an hour ago, she's showered and changed her clothes. She's now wearing a spring dress. It molds to all her curves. Curves I can't wait to explore. She spots me and pushes her glasses up her nose with a shy smile aimed my way.

My long legs eat up the distance between us.

"Hey, Ginny." I greet her with a kiss on her cheek.

Indigo raises her eyebrows. "Ginny? You never let anyone shorten your name before."

Ginny's cheeks darken. I can't wait to see how far her blush goes. Do her breasts turn pink when she's excited? My cock perks up at the idea. Although, to be fair, he's in a permanent state of almost excitement whenever Ginny's around.

"I'm not just anyone," I say with a wink.

Indigo laughs. "The gossip gals are right. This is fun."

"What's fun?" Cash asks as he joins us.

"Never you mind. Time to find our seats." She tugs him away.

"Shall we find our seats?" I ask Ginny once Indigo and Cash are gone.

"Our seats?" Her nose wrinkles. "I think we can sit anywhere."

"No, you can't," Sage yells from the other side of the room.

"Holy cow. How did she hear us?" Ginny whispers.

"I have excellent hearing," Sage answers.

"We also took a course on lip reading on the line," Cayenne adds.

Cash's half-brother, Peace, groans. "Tell me you didn't take a course in lip reading."

Clove grins at him. "Okay. We didn't take a course in lip reading."

"Forget what little privacy the residents of Winter Falls had. It's gone now," Peace mumbles.

Petal pats his arm. "It's cute you thought you had any privacy before."

Juniper claps her hands. "Are we ready for the movie?"

Olivia's hand shoots in the air. "Ten bucks says I know what the movie is."

Juniper scowls at her. "You do not know what the movie is."

"Please, it has to be *Forever My Girl*."

"We read the book," Feather adds. "The book is always better than the movie."

"I guess we'll find out," Olivia says. "Since we're watching the movie now."

"How did you know?" Juniper asks.

Olivia rolls her eyes. "It's a movie about a country star who returns to his hometown for a second chance at love." She nods to us.

I hold up my hands. "I'm not a country star."

"And this isn't our hometown," Ginny adds. Her voice is quiet but she speaks her mind and doesn't let anyone steamroll her. It's sexy as hell.

"But you both live in Winter Falls now and are in need of a second chance," Olivia explains.

"I think this movie was meant for me and Cash," Indigo says.

"Well, excuse me," Juniper grumbles. "I couldn't find a movie about a rockstar who humiliated a girl in high school but is now chasing her around like an adorable puppy."

"I am pretty adorable," I say.

Ginny slaps me. "It's not adorable to brag about being adorable."

I capture her hand and hold it to my chest.

"I wasn't bragging. I was merely stating a fact." I rub circles on her palm with my thumb and her breath catches. There goes another chip in her wall.

"This is my favorite project," Petal declares.

"Speaking of project." Sage points to the loveseat in the front room. "Your seat awaits, Dylan and Virginia."

I study the loveseat. It's barely big enough to hold my large frame. Ginny will have to sit real close in order for us both to fit. Perfect.

"Your chariot awaits, milady." I bow to Ginny and motion toward the seat.

She stares at me for a moment and I hold my breath. Did I push too fast? Will she turn me down in front of the entire town?

"Okay."

I keep hold of her hand as I lead her to the loveseat. I wait for her to sit before joining her. Her brow wrinkles when she realizes what a tight fit it is but she doesn't protest. Excellent.

"Here you go." Indigo drops a bucket of beer next to the chair and hands me a big bowl of popcorn.

"Thanks."

I hand Ginny the popcorn. "You want a beer?"

"Yes, please."

I open one for her before grabbing a bottle of my own.

Juniper clears her throat. "If the rockstar and librarian are ready now?"

I give Juniper a thumbs-up. "All ready."

The movie begins to play and I settle in. I wrap an arm around Ginny's shoulder. When she doesn't protest, I begin to play with the ends of her hair. It's not up in her typical bun today. The strands are smooth as silk. I bet they'd feel good fisted in my hand while she kneels before me.

Hell yeah. My cock is immediately on board. Thank goodness it's dark in here and Ginny can't see my erection. Just in case. I shift my beer to hide my crotch.

By the time the movie ends, Ginny is leaning into me. With her body pressed against mine, I can feel all of her curves. Curves I want to examine for myself. Touch and explore with my mouth and my hands.

The lights switch on and Ginny straightens before lifting her hands in the air to stretch her back. Her breasts jut forward and my mouth waters.

"I'm really not looking forward to moving all the furniture back."

I jump to my feet and offer her my hand. "I'll help."

But there's no need for our help. The attendees of the movie night are almost finished putting the tables and chairs back where they should be when the library opens in the morning.

"Huh. Why didn't Gratitude tell me the town would help? I could have had them help put everything in place before the movie, too."

"But then you wouldn't have seen me flexing my muscles."

I flex my bicep for her, and she giggles. It's a sound I want to hear every day for the rest of my life. I knew I wanted Ginny the second I saw her in the back room of the library, but the more I get to know her, the more I realize I want more than a few dates with her. I want all of her time.

Now to convince her to give me a chance.

I offer her my arm. "Shall I walk you home, Ms. Scott?"

She taps her chin as she contemplates for a few moments. The little minx is teasing me. After nearly a minute, she blows out a breath of air.

"I guess. Since we're going to the same apartment building and all, you may accompany me."

I wiggle my arm and she threads hers through mine.

"Do you need to lock up?"

"I got it!" Juniper jiggles a set of keys.

"What did you think of the movie?" I ask as we stroll down Main Street toward our apartment building.

"It was okay. But it was quite different than the book. The character names were all changed except for the main ones. And some of the background stories and character genders and business names were different."

"In other words, the book is better."

"You're learning. The book is always better."

We arrive at the apartment building and I unlock the door for her. When we reach her apartment, I want to lean down and kiss her. Guessing by the blush on her cheeks, she wouldn't mind. But kissing when we're friends and not dating is bulldozing. I'll wait until she has officially agreed to give me a chance.

"Good night, Ginny." I kiss her cheek before backing away.

"Good night," she mutters before rushing into her apartment.

I blow out a breath. If anticipation makes things sweeter, I may explode by the time I get my lips on hers.

Chapter 16

VIRGINIA

"Hey, Harry," I murmur as I remove my hedgehog from his cage. "How was your day?"

He does a little yawn since he's just waking up after having slept all day. Lucky hedgehog.

"Are you ready for some run around the house time?"

I swear at the word 'run' he perks up. Harry has a ton of energy. I would have a ton of energy if I slept twelve hours a day, too.

I set him down on the living room floor and he begins to zoom here, there, and everywhere. I sit on the floor, lean against the sofa, and watch him. This is my favorite way to spend time after a workday. I will never be a runner but watching little Harry zoom around the room? Totally relaxing.

After a while, my stomach rumbles. I stand and go to the kitchen in search of something to eat. The air is stifling in here. Colorado is having a bit of a heatwave today.

No one is allowed to have air-conditioning in town. It's banned since it's bad for the environment and everything bad for the environment is pretty much banned here. I don't mind. I can't afford the higher electricity bills anyway.

I open the window. Hopefully, I'll get a breeze flowing through the apartment.

A dog barks and I freeze. Harry's terrified of dogs. I glance behind me in time to catch him racing through the living room and down the hallway.

I chase after him as he dives under the bed. I search for him and discover him all rolled up in a protective ball as far away from me as possible.

"There's no reason to worry, little boy. The big bad doggy is far away and he can't get in here."

I continue to murmur reassurances to Harry, but he stays curled up in a protective ball. I check my watch and notice fifteen minutes have passed. After a scare, I can usually coax him out in five minutes.

I start to worry. I can't leave him under the bed all terrified. Poor little guy.

I creep out of the room before rushing out my front door to Dylan's apartment. I bang on the door until it's open.

"What's wrong?"

Water drips from Dylan's wet hair down his shoulders over his bare chest to the towel wrapped around his hips. He must have been in the shower and didn't have time to get dressed when I knocked.

Oh my. He's naked underneath that towel. How easy it would be to whip it off and have my wicked way with him.

"Ginny, what's wrong?"

His question snaps me out of my Dylan-sex-fog.

"It's Harry."

"Is he hurt? What happened?"

"He got scared and now he's hiding under the bed and won't come out. The last time he only needed five minutes before he calmed down but it's been fifteen and he's not coming out."

"Let me see what I can do."

He begins to stroll toward my apartment, but I stop him. Dylan in only a towel in my apartment is a temptation I won't be able to resist.

"Maybe you should get dressed first."

He glances down at his body. "If you insist," he says before rushing off.

He returns in a pair of cut-off sweats and nothing else. His glorious chest is still on display. I've always made fun of women and their obsession with six-pack abs. I was wrong. There's a lot to obsess about. A lot of skin to lick. A lot of ridges to explore.

"Let's go save Harry." Dylan grasps my hand and drags me across the hallway to my apartment. "He's hiding under the bed?"

At my nod, he leads me down the hallway to my bedroom. He starts to switch on the overhead light but I stop him.

"Bright light scares Harry."

"Then Harry won't have bright light. How about the lamp on your nightstand?"

I switch it on while Dylan gets to his knees. He sticks his head under the bed. "Hey Harry," he murmurs.

He lays on his stomach and crawls under the bed until his top half is hidden. I bite my tongue before I groan at how perfect his ass appears in those cut-offs. The shorts do nothing to hide how firm and round his muscles are.

What is wrong with me? Obsessing about a man's body while my hedgehog is in a crisis! I mentally slap myself as I make my way to the other side of the bed. I lay down on the floor and wiggle until my top half is under the bed.

Harry's still curled up at the end of the bed out of my reach. Poor little guy is scared to death. I don't blame him. Dogs are scary to me and they're not ten times my size.

"What happened, little man?" Dylan murmurs.

"Dog," I whisper.

"Did a big bad doggy scare you? Don't you worry. We'll stay right here with you until you aren't scared anymore."

My ovaries nearly explode at his words. I bet he'll speak to his children with the same gentle voice. He wouldn't let anything bad happen to his children. No one would bully them. And he certainly wouldn't treat them as if they're a nuisance. Not this guy.

"What should we talk about while we wait?" Dylan asks. I try to come up with a topic but he isn't asking me. "How about our days? You probably slept all day since you're nocturnal."

"How do you know hedgehogs are nocturnal?"

"I researched them after I found out about Harry."

I love how he doesn't play games. He's not pretending he knew everything about hedgehogs before he met me. Not Dylan. He's honest and open.

"I didn't sleep the day away the way you did, Harry. Nope. I spent the day at the recording studio. Jett was a big fat whiner all day long. Do you remember Jett? You bit him. Good taste by the way. He's a pain in the ass."

"What did he whine about?"

"What didn't he whine about is the question."

I giggle.

"But today wasn't all bad. I talked to my mom. She's doing well. She got a promotion at work. And my sister Stevie phoned. She got an A plus on a test."

"Do you talk to your sisters often?"

"At least once a week. We're close."

"Must be nice."

"You don't have any siblings?"

"I do. Two half-brothers." Two half-brothers I wish I'd never met. I haven't spoken to them since I left the house at eighteen.

"Half-brothers?"

"Same mom, different dad." What a relief. I wouldn't want my step-dad to be my real dad. Although to his sons, he's nice enough.

"Do you have a relationship with your dad?"

"He died when I was young."

"I'm sorry." He reaches across the carpet to squeeze my hand. "Why didn't you tell me before when we were discussing my dad?"

"Because we were discussing your dad."

"You're a very considerate person."

"Except for when someone humiliates me in high school."

"I am sorry. I didn't mean to humiliate you."

I squeeze his hand. "Not what I meant." I inhale a deep breath. "I'm sorry I was a total b-word to you."

"B-word?" He chuckles. "But seriously, you weren't a b-word or a c-word or any other word in the alphabet. I hurt you and I forgot. I still can't believe I don't remember you from high school."

"There isn't much to remember. I was a mouse."

"You're not a mouse," he grumbles. "Stop calling yourself one."

"I'm not the one who came up with the nickname."

"Teenagers are assholes."

As are step-dads and step-brothers.

"I'm sorry I wasn't friends with you in high school. I would've stopped all the assholes from calling you mean names."

"I know you would have."

"Hey! Look who's here." He releases my hand to capture Harry who's sniffing his armpit. "I just took a shower little guy. I promise."

He cuddles Harry to his chest before crawling out from underneath the bed.

That settles it. If Harry isn't afraid of Dylan, he has my stamp of approval. The next time he asks me out, I'll say yes.

"Come on, Harry. I'm sure your momma has a treat for you somewhere."

I wiggle out from under the bed and follow them to the kitchen. "He can have a bit of banana." I peel a banana and hand Dylan a small chunk.

His eyes sparkle with excitement. "Can I feed him?"

"He let you hold him. You can feed him."

"Do you use feeding tongs?"

I hand him the tongs. "You weren't kidding about doing your research."

He breaks off a tiny piece of banana and picks it up with the tongs before feeding it to Harry. It's a slow process but Dylan doesn't complain and bit by bit feeds him the small chunk.

"You're good with him."

"I like animals." He glances up at me with those ocean blue eyes and my breath nearly catches at the intensity in them. "Not to sound cliché, but I promise if you give me a chance, I'll treat you good, too."

Oh boy. I promised myself I'd say yes the next time he asked me out, but I didn't expect it to happen this soon. I inhale a deep breath to fortify myself.

"Okay."

"Okay?"

I nod. "Okay."

He whoops. "Awesome. I'm going to make our first date the best first date in the universe."

"You have your work cut out for you. I read a lot of romance books."

"Challenge accepted," he whispers before kissing my nose. "Thank you for giving me a chance."

And boom! Down go the walls I erected to keep Dylan Mitchell away from my heart.

I'm in big trouble here. Dylan's still a rockstar and I'm still a mouse. The pairing doesn't seem likely to last.

But a man who can talk my hedgehog out from under the bed is worth the risk.

Chapter 17

Obsession – wanting a woman with such a fierceness you don't care how much your bandmates tease you

DYLAN

"Okay," I say when we finish playing the song we're working on. "Good enough for today."

I don't wait for agreement from the rest of the band before whipping the guitar strap over my head and setting my guitar in its stand. It's time to go.

"What's wrong with you? Got ants in your pants?" Jett asks.

"Someone's got a date," Cash sings.

"Asshole," I mutter. He knows I don't want the band to find out about my date with Ginny.

"Virginia finally caved?" Gibson asks.

"Maybe he found a different woman willing to lower her standards for him," Jett says.

I flip him off before marching toward the door. "See ya."

"Where are you going?" Stan asks when I enter the sound room.

I'm about done with our producer. We were promised some time off after our last tour but instead, we're in Winter Falls recording an album. It's the slowest we've ever recorded before but still, we're not lounging around doing nothing all day.

"Have a good evening," I holler instead of giving Stan a piece of my mind.

"I didn't—"

Cash cuts him off. "Let it go. It's after five and we've been at it all day."

I hurry out of the room while Cash blocks Stan.

Once I'm back in my apartment, I take a quick shower and change. I grab the plant I bought as a gift since cut flowers are banned in Winter Falls and cross the hallway to Ginny's.

"Hey," she greets when she answers the door.

She's wearing another one of those spring dresses I love since they hug all her curves. And her hair is down showcasing how smooth and shiny it is. I want to touch those silk strands. Thread my hands through them as I explore her mouth.

My cock is immediately on board. He's had enough of my hand. He's ready for the real deal. Not the time.

I clear my throat and shove the plant at her. "This is for you."

Way to be smooth, Dylan. You're a freaking rockstar. There's nothing to be nervous about. Except this is Ginny. The woman I'm obsessed with. The woman I think could possibly be the one. The woman who doesn't give a damn about my fame.

"Thank you."

"Are you ready to go? Or do we need to let Harry out first?"

She pushes her glasses back up her nose. The nervous gesture makes me want to draw her into my arms and reassure her. "I'm ready. I already let Harry out for his hour of zooms."

"Hour of zooms?" I chuckle.

"Yeah, you know. Zooming here and there and everywhere."

She's adorable. And sweet and kind. And I can't wait to dirty her up. Those thoughts are not helping my cock to calm down.

I offer her my arm. "Your chariot awaits."

She sets the plant on the side table and grabs her purse before threading her arm through mine.

When we get outside, I point to the car. "Your chariot."

She gasps. "Holy cow. How much is this car worth? Maybe we should borrow one of the town's vehicles. This one is way too expensive."

She drags her feet but I pull her along. Note to self: Ginny is not impressed with wealth.

"This is Cash's car. I borrowed it for today."

"We don't need to drive anywhere. We can walk to the brewery or the diner or…"

I place a finger on her lips. "I promised you a date to remember."

She nods to the car. "I'm going to remember this."

"It's just a car."

"A car only the one percent can afford," she mumbles.

Good thing I didn't go with my first idea for this date – a dinner at this fancy Michelin-starred restaurant about an hour's drive away – she would not have been impressed.

I open the door and help her into the car. "Buckle up."

"I always do," she murmurs before I shut the door.

Hmm… another hint safety is a trigger for her. I need to figure out why but not now. All heavy subjects are off the table for today. Fun is on the agenda.

"Where are we going?" she asks once we're driving out of Winter Falls.

"It's a surprise."

She huffs but she doesn't beg me to tell her where we're going or whine. She's freaking perfect.

"How about a game?" she asks instead.

"Sure."

"Twenty questions."

"Twenty questions?" I glance over at her to wink. "You want to know twenty things about me? I'll confess everything."

She slaps my leg and I capture her hand. I place it on my thigh and cover my hand with it. I expect her to protest. But she doesn't. Good. She needs to get used to me touching her because I plan to touch her all the time.

"I think of a famous person and you get to ask twenty questions to figure out who it is."

"What do I get if I figure it out?"

"The satisfaction of a right answer."

I laugh. "Nope. How about a kiss instead?"

I notice her hand is shaking when she pushes her glasses up her nose. Did I push her too far?

"You won't win anyway." There's my girl. Backbone of steel hiding behind her shy exterior. There is literally nothing sexier in the world.

"But if I do?"

"Fine. A goodnight kiss."

I was planning on a goodnight kiss anyway, but now the anticipation will build inside her all night long. She's squirming in her seat already. Perfect.

"Do you have a person in mind?"

"I do." She grins. It's cute she thinks she's already won. I'll let her believe it for a little while.

"Am I alive?"

"No."

"Am I a woman?"

"Yes."

"Am I a writer?"

"Yes."

I could continue to ask more questions until I've hit the twenty allotted but winning is more fun.

"Am I Jane Austen?"

She gasps. "How did you know?"

"You have the special hardback editions of all her books on her bookshelf."

"How do you know what books are on my bookshelf?"

"I pay attention." Which is a very nice way of saying I've been obsessed with her since I first saw her in the library appearing all prim and proper with a pencil sticking out of her hair.

"You're a cheater." She pulls her hand away from my thigh to cross her arms over her chest.

"I'm a cheater? Or you're a sore loser?"

She harrumphs.

"I didn't figure my little librarian would be a sore loser," I tease.

"I'm not a sore loser. You're a cheater."

I chuckle. "Not sure how I could cheat. I'm not a vampire. I can't read your mind."

She narrows her eyes at me. "How do I know you're not a vampire? It kind of makes sense. You're wealthy. Tick. You lured me into a date with you. Tick. You're gorgeous. Tick."

"You think I'm gorgeous?" Damn. I wish I wasn't driving. I wish I could press her against a wall and make her admit what she thinks about me.

"You have a mirror. You know you're gorgeous." She sniffs and lifts her nose in the air.

I groan. Her prim and proper routine is sexy as hell. It makes me hard every time the librarian in her makes an appearance.

"And you're beautiful."

"You don't have to flatter me. I honor my bets. You'll get your goodnight kiss."

"I'm not lying. You are beautiful. You knocked me off my feet the first time I saw you. Again. The first time I saw you again."

Way to go, idiot. Way to remind her of how you didn't notice her in high school.

She giggles. "You ran into a wall."

"You're lucky I didn't get hurt and sue you."

"Ah, I wouldn't want you to harm your looks. Since you don't have anything else going for you."

"Maybe I should have my face insured. Just in case."

"Are you planning to run into another wall?"

I shrug. "With you around looking all beautiful, who knows what'll happen."

"And the tabloids claim Gibson's the charmer."

I nearly ask her if she reads the tabloids about the band but snap my mouth shut before I make another colossal blunder. Reminding her of my fame and how much money I have is not the way to Ginny's heart. And make no mistake about it. My goal is to capture her heart.

"We're here," I say when I pull into the parking lot.

"A bookstore?" She gasps. "You brought me to a bookstore?"

"No. I brought you on a tour of bookstores. I read this town has more bookstores per capita than any other place in Colorado."

She launches herself over the console and into my arms. "Thank you!"

I wrap my arms around her. "You're welcome, Ginny."

Her lips meet mine in a barely there kiss. More a peck than an actual kiss. But it's enough to get a taste of her. She tastes of sunshine and summer days. I want more.

"This doesn't count as our goodnight kiss."

She bites her bottom lip as she studies me.

"Does this?" She presses her lips to mine. They're soft and smooth. I thread my hands through her hair the way I've been dreaming about since I first saw her. She gasps and I use the opportunity to slip my tongue into her mouth.

Sunshine and summer days. Who knew the taste would be this appealing? My tongue explores her mouth but Ginny isn't an innocent bystander. Her tongue meets mine. It's tentative at first but the more I stroke into her mouth, the bolder she becomes.

I readjust her until she's straddling my lap. She moans when she feels my hard length. It's all for her.

I trail my free hand along her side until I reach the underside of her breast. She arches her back and—

Honk!

She yanks her lips away from me – the spell of our kiss broken by the car horn. Her eyes are wide and concerned as she scans the parking lot.

I grasp her chin and force her to meet my gaze. "No one's looking."

"You didn't even check. I thought you weren't a vampire."

"I don't need to look. We're in a parking lot with no cars nearby." I never park near other cars. Safety protocol rule number one when you're famous.

"Okay."

"You're okay?"

She nods.

"Good because I still want a goodnight kiss."

"It's good to have goals," she teases before crawling to her side of the car and opening the door. "Come on. There are books to be bought."

I readjust my cock in my jeans before I follow her. I was already obsessed with my little librarian. But now I've tasted her and experienced her teasing? My obsession is only growing.

Chapter 18

Virginia

"Did you reshelve those books I asked you to?" Gratitude asks.

She asked me to do those books less than five minutes ago. What does she think? I'm a magician who can magically transport books throughout the library while sitting next to her? Please. If I was a magician, I wouldn't waste my talent on moving books through a library.

I inhale a deep breath and paste a smile on my face. "I'll do it now."

I pick up the pile of books and walk off before she can order me to do more work right now when it can clearly wait.

I don't know why she doesn't like me. I'm easy to get along with. I do my work without complaint. I come in on time every day. I stay late if necessary. But no matter what I do, she's a complete grump to me. Maybe she's just a grumpy woman?

I return to the circulation desk determined to ask Gratitude if I've somehow offended her. But the door opens and Dylan strolls in with a tray of coffees.

He smirks and my body warms. I remember how those lips felt on mine. How he made me feel as if he couldn't get enough of my mouth, my taste. I know I couldn't get enough of him. I doubt I ever will.

I was tempted to throw all my good girl ways out the window and ask him inside my apartment last night. I almost did. It was actually Dylan who backed off and wished me good night before walking away.

"Hey, Ginny." He kisses my cheek. "How is your day going?"

"Better now."

He smirks. "Seeing me makes everything better?"

"I was referring to the coffee." I snag a mug from the tray and take a sip to hide my amusement at his offended face.

"I'll blow you away with the cupcake I brought you."

I widen my eyes and mouth *no*.

Gratitude will lose her mind if she catches me eating a cupcake in the library. Drinks are allowed but food isn't. I can't even eat at my desk in the office. I have to eat outside. Otherwise, the crumbs from my apparently messy eating will attract rodents and then they will destroy all the books and probably burn the place down while they're at it.

"Young man," Gratitude begins. Uh oh. Here we go.

"Don't you worry," Dylan says as he approaches her. "I brought you a coffee and treat, too."

Gratitude's mouth opens but she seems to have lost the ability to speak.

Dylan places the mug on the desk in front of her. "Caramel latte. A little birdie told me it's your favorite."

He winks and she blushes. Now my mouth's hanging open. How in the world did Dylan charm the grumpy librarian in two seconds flat?

"I also brought you a piece of cheesecake. Bryan said it's your secret favorite. Don't worry. I won't tell anyone."

Gratitude doesn't hesitate to snatch the cheesecake from him. "I'm on break," she says as she hurries out the front door of the library.

What just happened?

Dylan places a finger under my jaw to shut my mouth. "What's with the gaping?"

"I can't believe you charmed Gratitude. She hates me."

"She doesn't hate you. She wouldn't have hired you if she hated you."

"She didn't hire me. The town did. I didn't even meet her when I visited for the interviews. She was having lunch at the diner when I toured the library." I pause as I come to a realization. "She never has lunch at the diner. I think I was conned."

"She'll warm to you eventually. How can she resist your charm?"

I snort. "You're the charming one."

"Come on. Let's have our treats."

"We can't eat in the library."

He ignores me and sits down at a table. He places our cupcakes on it before digging napkins out of his pockets.

"I'm serious. We can't eat in the library."

"Don't worry." He winks. "I know the librarian."

"I'm not the librarian yet. She can still fire me."

And then what would I do? I moved my entire life to Winter Falls. This is my dream. A small town where I can get to know the people. People who never knew me as the mouse.

"If she didn't hire you, she can't fire you."

I don't believe him, but I hate to argue. What I will do is research my contract later.

"What are you doing here anyway?" I ask as I sit across from him. He slides the cupcake across the table at me but I ignore it.

"We quit recording early. One of Jett's sticks broke and he had a temper tantrum."

I raise my eyebrows. "A temper tantrum?"

Dylan shrugs. "Everyone has short fuses these days. We haven't had a break in ages. We finished our last tour and arrived in Winter Falls the next day."

"No vacation in Bali or somewhere else exotic?"

"I'm not much of a beach guy."

"No?" I sigh. "I could spend a week on the beach soaking up the sun while reading books and drinking pina coladas."

"Huh. When you put it that way, I understand the appeal."

"You do? You're going to spend the day reading and drinking pina coladas from a pineapple?"

"Nope." He grins. "I'm going to spend the day ogling you while you lounge in a little red bikini."

"Nope. No way. No how. I don't wear bikinis."

"Now, you're being cruel."

"I'm being cruel for not wearing a bikini?"

"You're ruining my daydream of studying every single curve on your body during the day on the beach before spending the night discovering those curves with my hands and mouth."

My body heats and warmth spreads to my core where wetness gathers. I rub my thighs together to relieve some of the tension. I'm totally down with him spending the night exploring my body. Assuming I can explore his, too.

I'd start with those ab muscles I've been fantasizing about since I caught him in nothing but a towel. Or maybe I'll explore his tattoos with my tongue. Or I could go old school and start with a kiss.

There's a bang on the door. When I glance over, Gibson and Jett give us two thumbs-up each. Dylan flips them off and they laugh.

"I don't know. Does this fantasy include us getting away from your bandmates?" I ask once the two clowns are gone.

"Don't worry. Jett and Gibson snap their fingers and women come running. We'd be rid of them soon enough."

I frown. For a minute there I forgot all about how Dylan's in a band. And not any old band. A band that tours the world playing their number one hits to women who scream their never-ending devotion to them while throwing their panties at the stage.

"I was joking. I would never invite Jett and Gibson on a vacation with us."

"I know. I know. Ignore me."

"Nope. I know you hate confrontation."

I scowl at him. How does he know I don't enjoy confrontation? Maybe he really can read minds.

"Are you certain you're not a vampire?"

"I can't read your mind, Ginny. But I do pay attention and you avoid confrontation even when it's blatantly apparent you have an issue."

"Blatantly apparent?"

"Being in a rock band doesn't make me dumb. I can say big words."

"I know." I fiddle with my mug for a while before I admit what's bothering me. "I worry about the whole rock band thing."

"Worry? Worry about what? I promise the one bar fight Cash and I were in was the only fight. And I didn't break the TV. It fell off the stand when Jett slammed my door. And—"

I raise a hand to stop him. Naming all of his adventures is not helping the situation.

"Never mind. It's silly."

"Nothing you think about or worry about is silly."

He always knows the exact right thing to say. "I should send your mom a bouquet of roses to thank her. She did right when she raised you."

He grins. "She did but you're not changing the subject."

"You're like a hedgehog with a maze. Never gonna give up."

"Nope. I have stamina." He waggles his eyebrows.

"I give up." I throw my arms in the air. "You're a rockstar and I'm a librarian."

He waits for me to explain further, but when I don't he says, "I'm aware."

"Then, you're also aware how this idea of us dating is crazy. You're famous and I'm a mouse."

He growls. "Say mouse one more time and I'm putting you over my knee and spanking you until you promise to never say the word again."

I forget how to breathe. He wants to spank me? Would I be naked? Would he? Would he get me all excited and then— What is wrong with me? I don't enjoy being spanked. I think.

No wondering about being spanked. I'm in the middle of work. In a library!

"What if I'm discussing an actual mouse Indigo's devil cat chased around town? Can I say mouse then?"

"You're just begging for me to bend you over my knee." He growls and I melt. This is what those romance heroines mean when they say their entire body quivers with excitement.

"You are not a mouse. Whoever made you feel bad about yourself was jealous of you and lashing out about their own insecurities."

"Now you're a psychologist."

He shrugs. "I enjoy reading. Being on the road in a tour bus for days on end gets boring."

He's adorable when he's embarrassed. Gah! Can this man be less appealing, please?

"Yes, I'm a rockstar, but I'm also just a man. An ordinary man. I mean a gorgeous man but still a man who puts his pants on one leg at a time."

"Unless you're wearing a towel," I mumble.

He grins. Darn it! Why did I open my mouth and basically confess to ogling him?

He reaches across the table to grasp my hand. "Fame isn't real. You are. I am. Don't let the fame stuff stop us from becoming something great."

"Something great?"

"I always aim for the stars." He squeezes my hand. "Let's take it day by day. Whenever you have a concern about my fame, we can discuss it."

He's good. Really good. And I'm being weak. Afraid he'll run off on me because he's famous and I'm a mou— librarian. I promised myself I wouldn't be weak anymore when I left home. I promised I'd try new things. Not hold back.

"Okay. Day by day."

"Day by day."

He smiles and his dimple comes out. Alarm bells ring in my mind. It would be so easy to fall in love with this man.

"Now, the heavy's done. How about I accompany you into the stacks where we pretend we're teenagers and make out?"

He waggles his eyebrows and I giggle. He makes me feel like a teenager. But not a teenager who was bullied by her peers. One of those popular girls who was always getting caught in the library with some football player.

Those alarm bells are no longer ringing. No, they're blaring as loud as they can. This man is a danger to my heart. But when those blue eyes and dimple are aimed at me, I find it hard to care.

Chapter 19

DYLAN

"Are you ready?" I ask Ginny when she opens her door.

"I'm not sure what I should be ready for. The last Winter Falls festival was crazy."

I grin. "It was fun."

"Except I was a b-word to you when you asked me out."

I tweak her nose. "I thought we agreed you have never been nor ever will be a b-word."

She giggles. "It sounds silly when you say b-word."

"I'll agree to never say b-word again if you do the same."

She glares at me. "You're tricky."

"Only when I have to be."

She blows out a breath of air. "I'll try."

"All I can ask." I offer her my arm. "Shall we?"

"Do you know what Beltane is?" I ask once we're strolling toward the festival.

"I researched it since I want to stay in Winter Falls."

"And?" I prompt when she doesn't continue.

"Beltane is the celebration of the peak of spring and the coming summer. The name Beltane is a derivative from Belenus, the Celtic sun god. It's strongly associated with fertility."

"Fertility?"

She shrugs. "Don't ask me. I don't know how a town celebrates fertility."

Thanks to having Gibson and Jett in my life, I have a few ideas. None of which are remotely appropriate.

"It's nice how everything's close in Winter Falls," I say when we reach Main Street a few minutes later.

"You're not bored in a small town?"

I motion toward the people enjoying the festival. "What's there to be bored about?"

Ginny pulls on my hand to stop me from joining the crowd. "Shouldn't you be in disguise?"

"In disguise?"

"After what happened at the Eostre Festival." She scans the crowd as if searching for fans waiting to pop out and rush me. It's adorable.

"They recognized Cash. He's the face of the band. Thus, the name *Cash & the Sinners*. No one will recognize me."

She worries her bottom lip between her teeth. As much as I want to play with her lip, I need to reassure her more. I don't want her worried. Especially after she finally confessed her fears about me being a rockstar while she's a 'lowly' librarian.

There's nothing lowly about Virginia Hale. But it's going to take time to convince her otherwise. She's worth the effort.

"How about I put on a hat?" I dig the ballcap I always carry with me out of my back pocket and put it on. "What do you think? I'm sexy, aren't I? The question is. Am I too sexy?"

She giggles. I want to spend my life making her giggle. There are other things I want to spend my life making her do but patience is the name of the game.

"Uh oh," she mutters and points.

The gossip gals are approaching. I love these women. Are they over the top? Yes, they are. But they're also on a mission to match me with Ginny. I'll take whatever help I can get.

"You're late," Sage says.

"Late? I didn't realize we had a date." I chuckle. "I'm a poet and didn't know it."

Ginny groans. "Mr. Cliché has arrived at the party."

"Don't be silly. Mr. Cliché is always at the party."

"You need to hurry or you'll miss the Maypole dance."

The Maypole dance sounds fun.

"Um, I don't want to dance." Ginny's shoulders drop and she hunches forward. She's trying to disappear, but I won't stand for it. She should shine bright.

"But you'll miss a whole year of fertility if you don't dance around the Maypole," Cayenne exclaims.

Ginny's eyes widen as she retreats a step. "A whole year of fertility?"

I guess we now know how a festival celebrates fertility. I wouldn't mind Ginny ensuring she's fertile for a year. I can imagine little girls with Ginny's long brown hair and her whiskey colored eyes running around at our feet. I've always wanted a big family.

But it's too early. We've barely started dating and Ginny still has reservations about me being in a rock band.

I clasp Ginny's hand to keep her from fleeing. "If Ginny doesn't want to do the Maypole dance, you won't force her."

Clove sighs. "Ginny? He calls her Ginny."

Petal smiles. "Wonderful. Our plan is working."

Sage crosses her arms over her chest. "Our plan was to get them to dance around the Maypole."

Feather winks at me. "I love surprise pregnancy books."

Ginny squeaks. Her fear is palpable in the air. As much as I'm enjoying the matchmaking by the gossip gals, I won't have Ginny scared.

"We're not dancing around the Maypole. The decision is final."

Feather fans her face with her hand. "Oh my. He does have a bit of alpha in him."

Cayenne rolls her eyes. "Of course, he does. He's her protector."

"If you'll excuse us, ladies. I promised my girl a hot chocolate." I don't wait for them to respond before steering Ginny through the crowd toward the stand set up in front of *Bake Me Happy*.

"Thank you," Ginny says.

"I haven't bought you the hot chocolate yet." I wink to let her know I understand her, but she doesn't need to thank me for protecting her. She never will.

"But you will."

No sense denying it. She doesn't know it yet but I'll buy her whatever she wants.

"Virginia!" Bryan shouts in greeting when we reach the front of the line. "I haven't seen you in a while."

She ducks her head. Why is she embarrassed?

"Two hot chocolates, please," I order despite how wonderful the weather is on this first day of May. I know Ginny loves her hot chocolate.

"I love this." Bryan claps. "You two are adorable together." He hands me the drinks. "I'm finally going to win a bet."

I scowl. As much as I enjoy the gossip gals matchmaking us, I don't approve of the corresponding betting.

Bryan wags a finger at me. "If you think your scowl is discouraging, you haven't looked in a mirror lately."

I hand Virginia her drink and pay him before steering us toward a bench in front of the community center where we can sit and drink our hot chocolates.

"What did Bryan mean about not seeing you lately? You love *Bake Me Happy*."

Whenever I bring her a treat or a drink from the bakery, her eyes light with excitement. Which is why I do it as often as I can. Watching her eyes light with excitement is my new drug and I'm addicted.

She pushes her glasses up her nose before answering. "It's not a big deal. I'm trying to save money is all."

I clear my throat before I growl. I understand saving money and cutting corners to get by, but she has a good job. She should be able to afford a treat from the bakery.

"Is there anything in particular you're saving your money for?"

"A house." She stares into the distance. "I've always wanted a house of my own. Where I can choose the furniture, the decorations. Where I have control."

There's more to it than picking out furniture but pushing Ginny won't get me anywhere.

"I believe in you. You'll get your house."

She smiles up at me. Her whole face alight with happiness. Yep. Not pushing her was the right decision.

We sit in silence enjoying our drinks until music blares from the speakers.

"Am I hearing things or is that the song *Zombie?*" she asks.
"It is. What's going on?"

"Let's go check it out."

I offer her my hand and we follow the music until we reach the town square where a large Maypole is set up. Gibson and Jett have joined in on the fun and are holding onto colored ribbons while dancing around the pole.

"Should we tell them it's a fertility ritual?" she asks.

"It's no fun if we don't tell them."

"I don't know. It's pretty fun watching them skip around like a bunch of deranged merrymakers."

"Trust me. This will be even more fun." I raise my voice and shout, "Hey, Jett." He waves when he spots me. "How many children are you hoping to have next year?"

He stumbles. "Children?"

Jett's afraid of having his own children. It doesn't stop him from being a man whore, though.

I indicate the Maypole. "It's a fertility ritual."

He squeals and drops the ribbon. He also halts in his tracks causing Gibson to run into him. They fall in a pile on the ground. Ginny bursts into laughter.

"You're right," she says when she catches her breath. "Telling them was funnier."

Her smile and lips beckon me. I don't bother trying to resist. Why would I?

I lean down and press my lips to hers. She opens her mouth and I slip my tongue inside. Her taste of sunshine and summer days hits me and I growl before deepening the kiss.

Ginny's right there with me. She clutches my shoulders and pulls me close until our bodies collide. Someone jostles her from behind and I wrap my arms around her to protect her before slowing the kiss.

I glance down at her swollen lips and wide eyes. I want to enjoy her this way every day for the rest of my life. I'm falling for this woman. She's it. The person I've been searching for. Now to convince her of the same.

Chapter 20

Sexy book club – an excuse to discuss sex and all things smutty

VIRGINIA

"What are you doing here?" I ask Indigo when I open my door to find her standing in the hallway.

She waggles her eyebrows. "Expecting someone else?"

No. Not expecting. Hoping maybe. Although Dylan messaged to let me know the band is recording late tonight. My heart did this whole romance heroine galloping thing when he messaged to 'just let me know'.

"Put your shoes on. We're going out."

I scowl at her. "You know I don't enjoy going out."

"You'll enjoy this," she sings.

I cross my arms over my chest. "I will?"

"Yep."

"I'm not going anywhere until you tell me what we're doing."

I've learned my lesson. One adventure to Chinatown for some special sweet and sour sauce she couldn't find anywhere else in San Diego was enough for me. Trust me. There's a reason no one else sells that sauce.

"It's sexy book club night."

The gossip gals mentioned a book club but I wasn't sure if I believed them since they were talking about strippers at the time. I guess book club isn't a figment of their imagination after all.

"How did you find out about a book club?"

"It's on the Winter Falls Facebook group page."

I wrinkle my nose. Social media is not my thing. Not considering my bullies used it to harass me as a teenager when school wasn't in session. Thanks, Mark Zuckerberg, for developing a means for bullies to continue their bullying even when you think you're safe at home.

"Still not on social media?" Indigo asks.

"It doesn't matter." I'm not discussing this with her. She thinks I need to 'let it go already'. "I can't go to book club anyway."

"Why not?"

"I didn't know about book club, so I haven't read the book." And I don't go to book club without reading the book. I actually feel it should be a rule. No entry if you haven't finished reading the book!

She grins. "I bet you have."

"Fine. I'll bite. What book is it?"

"*Obsession Falls.*"

I glare at her. "No fair. You cheated."

She widens her eyes. "How did I cheat?"

"You know I'm obsessed with Claire Kingsley." The Miles Family series hooked me and I haven't let go since.

"You're out of excuses. Let's go."

I narrow my eyes. "How am I out of excuses? You didn't bother to ask if I have any plans."

"One, your boyfriend is busy. Two, you never have plans."

"Dylan isn't my boyfriend." We've been on two dates. Two dates does not a boyfriend make.

"Dylan is totally your boyfriend."

"Whatever." I'm not going to fight her on this. She's been pushing me toward Dylan since he arrived in town. I don't know why. She's usually not pushy. Unless… "Did you place a bet on me and Dylan getting together?"

"Me?" She feigns being innocent but when she cracks her knuckles I know she's lying.

"You know I hate betting." She's one of the few people who knows why.

"It's a bit of innocent fun. It's not malicious. Everyone in town wants you two together is all."

"I don't know if I want to live in the same town as you anymore."

She bounces on her toes. "You love me and you know it."

"I should have transferred high schools," I mumble as I slip on my shoes and grab my keys.

"Don't forget your Kindle."

I grab my purse and slam the door. "You won. You can stop gloating now."

She laces her arm through mine. "Don't be silly. The gloating has only just begun."

"Where is book club anyway?" I ask to head off the gloating since Indigo is an excellent gloater. Ask me how I know.

"Sexy book club," she corrects.

I roll my eyes. "Where is sexy book club?"

"*Fall Into A Good Book.*"

"The bookstore your grandma used to own?" I don't know why I'm asking. There's only one bookstore in town. Considering the size of the town, it's lucky there's a bookstore at all. Although, judging by how busy the library is, the townspeople love to read.

"Yep. A local bought it. Aspen is her name. She's married to the chief of police."

I haven't met Aspen yet despite visiting the bookstore a few times. I probably should make more of an effort to make friends in town since I plan to stay here.

But making friends hasn't been easy for me since sixth grade when I became friends with Julie only to find out later her other friends bet her she couldn't make friends with the 'shy bookworm'. Merely one of the reasons I hate betting.

We reach the bookstore and Indigo opens the door to usher me inside. I stall when I notice how crowded it is. Crowds make me nervous. This was a bad idea. I back up but Indigo nudges me forward until I stumble inside.

"Welcome to the sexy book club," a woman greets us. "I'm Aspen."

I hold out my hand. "I'm—"

"Virginia, the new librarian."

"If Gratitude ever retires," I grumble.

She laughs. "Gratitude is a force of nature. She hated me when we were kids."

"Probably because you used to hide in the dark corners to make out with Lyric," someone from behind her mutters.

Aspen beams. "It's true." She waves her left hand at me. "Lyric and I are married now."

"Gag." The woman behind her feigns throwing up.

"Ignore my sister. It's what I do." She motions to the chairs set in a circle. "Find a seat. There's wine and nibbles at the bar."

I raise my eyebrows. "Bar?"

"It's not really a bar. It's the check-out counter."

Someone hollers her name and she bustles away.

Indigo steers me toward the bar. "Aren't you glad you came now?"

My stomach rumbles in agreement. I didn't have a chance to eat dinner yet. I scan the bar laden with food. I'm glad I haven't eaten.

I make a plate of cheese, sausage, and crackers and grab a bottle of beer.

"Let's sit there." Indigo points to two chairs near the door.

Darn it. Now, I can't be mad at her. She knows I'm uncomfortable and want to be near the exit in case I need to escape.

The door bangs open and Sage marches in followed by the rest of the gossip gals. "Sorry we're late."

I tuck my chin into my chest and concentrate on my food before they spot me. I do not want to know what they're up to now. Those women scare the snot out of me.

"It wasn't my fault," Feather insists.

"You're the one who forgot to buy the fabric paint," Clove points out.

"At least I didn't wash the sweatshirts in itchy fabric softener," Feather says.

Petal holds up her hands. "Don't bring me into this."

"It's okay," Aspen greets them. "We haven't begun yet."

"Good." Sage nods. "You ready, gossip gals?" At their nod, she counts down. "Three, two, one."

They open their sweaters to reveal bright pink t-shirts with the saying *I read smut. What's your superpower?* on them.

"I want one of those."

"Oh good. You're here," Sage says and I realize I spoke aloud. Great. The gossip gals are zeroed in on me now.

"I'll make you a t-shirt," Cayenne says.

Sage holds up a hand. "We'll discuss t-shirts later. First, I want to know what's holding you back."

I point to myself. "Me?"

"Yes, you."

I have no idea what she's talking about. "Holding me back from what?"

"Dylan."

"I'm not holding back from Dylan. We're dating."

"But you haven't had sex yet."

I gasp. "How do you know?"

Sage chuckles. "Because you just confirmed it." She holds out her hand to Cayenne. "You owe me ten bucks."

Cayenne scowls as she slaps a bill in Sage's palm. "I don't know how you're holding out. Dylan is one sexy man."

He is. And I've been sorely tempted. But I'm a good girl. I don't jump into bed with men I don't know.

Although, I have known Dylan for decades. And he's friends with Indigo. A woman I would jump off a cliff for if she asked me to. She's been pushing me to hook up with Dylan for a while. She'd never steer me wrong. Hmm…. Maybe sex with Dylan should be an option sooner rather than later.

"Good. She's thinking about it. Now, can we discuss the book?" Feather asks.

Clove moans. "She always wants to discuss the book."

"This is a book club."

"It's sexy book club," Cayenne points out. "There's lots of hot sex, the couple fight, they get back together again. The end."

"I don't know," I start and everyone turns their attention to me. Gah! Why did I open my mouth? "We could discuss why Josiah was solitary. Why he didn't want a woman in his life."

"Because he's a protector the same as your Dylan," Feather says. "He couldn't help himself."

I try really, really hard not to respond. I know she's baiting me. But I can't help myself. I feel my face go soft. Dylan is my protector. He's not a bully forcing his will on me. He's the man standing beside me holding my hand and making sure no one gets too close to hurt me.

Oh boy. I'm falling for Dylan. I knew I would if I opened myself up to him. It's why I tried to keep a wall around my heart. It didn't work.

If he had come at me with a sledgehammer, my wall would still be intact. But he didn't. He chipped away at it until it fell.

Until I fell.

Chapter 21

Invite inside – when a goodnight kiss isn't enough

DYLAN

Cash's phone beeps. "Time to go," he says after reading the message. "Indy's done with book club."

I stand. "I'll join you."

Ginny texted me earlier tonight to let me know she was at book club with Indigo. I love how she took the initiative to let me know where she was. It means she's learning to trust me.

By the time we're back on tour, I want her used to messaging me. I don't want to worry about where she is. I'll worry enough about how she's doing. I don't need to worry about where she is as well.

Cash chuckles. "I thought you would."

We pack up our instruments and wave to our sound technician before taking off. Gibson and Jett turn left toward the *Naked Falls Brewery,* and Fender heads home while Cash and I make our way to the bookstore.

We reach *Fall into A Good Book* and wait while Indigo and Ginny say goodbye to everyone. Indigo steps outside, notices Cash, and jumps into his arms.

Ginny smiles at them before she notices me. She pushes her glasses up her nose. "Hi."

She's adorable when she's shy. She's pretty much adorable all the time. Good thing she doesn't realize she can push her glasses up her nose, ask me for anything, and it's hers. Who am I kidding? I don't care. She can have whatever she wants.

I tag her hand and pull her near. I press my lips to hers in a hard fast kiss. "Hi," I whisper against her mouth.

"Your hi was better." Her cheeks flush when she realizes what she said. Again. Adorable.

The bell above the door to the bookstore jingles and she steps away from me. "What are you doing here?"

"I came to walk you home. I don't want you walking home alone in the dark."

"Indigo's here."

I point to Cash and Indigo who are now making out. "I don't think she'll be walking you home."

"Those two never could keep their hands off each other."

Her words are wistful as if she too wishes for a man who can't keep his hands off of her. Don't you worry, Ginny. I'm here and my hands want to be on you all the time.

"They were pretty disgusting in high school," I say instead of confessing my desires.

She rolls her eyes. "So disgusting."

"You ready to go home or do you have another engagement this evening?"

She motions down the street. The dark street where all the stores have already closed up for the evening. Even the diner and coffee shop are closed. Only the brewery and bar are open past ten in this town.

It sounds dull, but Winter Falls is anything but dull. It would be a good place to raise children. If a particular woman wants children.

I grasp her hand and we begin walking home. "Do you want children?"

"I do. I want a big family. Kids running around everywhere. No one yelling at them to be quiet."

I frown. This isn't the first time she's hinted about her home life being troubled during her childhood. I want to know everything about it. And I will. In time.

"I want a big family, too."

"You do?" She glances up at me.

"Yep. I love visiting my sister, Janis. Did I tell you she has two boys? Her house is complete chaos. But there's love."

She sighs. "Sounds wonderful."

Giving Ginny a family just went to the top of the list of things I want to give her. Not the top, top. First, a house.

We reach our apartment complex and walk up the stairs to her apartment. I want to follow her inside and show her how I feel about her. But I'm not rushing her. I'll settle for a goodnight kiss.

Ginny opens her door before glancing up at me from beneath her lashes. Her glasses slide down her nose and she pushes them up with both hands.

"Do you want to come inside?"

I step closer. "For a coffee?"

"I can't sleep if I drink coffee this late."

"For a nightcap?"

"I don't have any hard liquor in my house."

I was wrong. A house isn't the first thing I want to give Ginny. I want to give her orgasms – lots and lots of orgasms – first. I close in on her until she's trapped against the wall. "What would we do if I came inside?"

Her breath catches and her breasts rub against my chest. "I'm sure we could think of something."

"Are you sure?" I tuck a strand of hair behind her ear. "I don't want to rush you."

"I'm sure."

I thread my hand through her hair. "You won't regret it in the morning?"

"I won't regret it in the morning."

I gaze into her eyes. I can't detect anything but honesty in those whiskey eyes. Honesty is good but I want to see her eyes overcome with passion.

"Promise?"

"I promise I won't regret inviting you inside my apartment to watch television."

"Oh, you've got jokes now, do you?"

She giggles and I can't resist tasting those lips. Feeling them press against mine. Plunging my tongue into her mouth to explore each and every crevice. She moans and I stroke into her mouth to give her more. To give her everything.

When I run out of breath, I pull away and lean my forehead against hers. "Your taste is addicting."

"Good. The label didn't lie then."

Damn. She's fun. I shut the door and make sure it's locked before picking her up.

"Stop! I'm too heavy."

I bobble her and she squeals.

"You're not heavy. My guitar weighs more than you."

We enter her bedroom and I lay her on the bed. I switch on the bedside light. I'd prefer the overhead light to allow me to study every inch of her body without shadows but Ginny's a shy thing. A bright light will make her uncomfortable. We'll work up to it.

I cover her with my body. "Is Harry okay or should I move him into the living room?"

"Are you worried Harry's going to observe and score your technique?"

I remove her glasses and place them on the nightstand. I want to be able to gaze into her eyes while I'm buried deep inside her. "Don't you worry, my little librarian, I'll score tens in all techniques."

Heat flares in her eyes. "All techniques?"

"Mouth." I kiss her lips. "Hands." I glide the back of my hand up her arm. "And cock." I press my hard length against her stomach.

"I-I-I." She swallows. "I think I need a demonstration of these so-called techniques."

"Your wish is my command." I wink. "But first things first. You're wearing entirely too many clothes."

She grabs the hem of her t-shirt but I capture her wrist before she can move. "Nuh-uh. I'll be the one removing your clothes this evening."

She nods and I drop her wrist. "If anything I do bothers you or scares you, say the word and I'll stop."

"What are you going to do that's scary? Grow a tentacle and use it to…" She pauses. "Touch me."

I chuckle. I know exactly where she meant by 'touch me'. "A tentacle?"

"I enjoy reading sci-fi romance."

"I think I need to examine your book collection closer."

"Why?" She cocks a brow. "Do you need hints on technique?"

"There's one."

"One what?"

"One session in orgasm denial." She gasps. "Don't worry. You'll enjoy it."

"The word denial doesn't usually equate with enjoy."

"Just you wait and see."

"Promises. Promises."

I don't bother responding with words. It's time to respond with deeds. I grasp the hem of her t-shirt. I make sure to glide my hands over her torso as I lift the material up and over her body leaving her in her bra. Her white, lacy bra.

I trace a finger along the edge of the material. I smirk as goosebumps appear in my wake. I've always been a breast man and Ginny's are spectacular. Almost more than a handful. Good thing I have big hands.

I need to touch her skin. I remove her bra and throw it over my shoulder. I massage her breasts and her head falls back as she arches into my hands with a moan. Her nipples form hard peaks.

"I can't wait to fuck these," I murmur. "But not tonight."

Tonight, I want to feel her pussy surrounding me, squeezing me. My cock twitches at the idea. He's ready. Not yet. I plan to make Ginny out of her mind with desire before I finally sink into her.

I trail my hand down her chest until I reach her jeans. I snap them open and draw down the zipper. Her breath hitches. I could become addicted to the sound.

I play with the bow on the front of her white panties. The bow and the white make her appear innocent. I can't wait to dirty her up.

I draw her jeans and panties down her legs and she helps by kicking them off. I stand and remove my t-shirt. She reaches for her glasses.

"What are you doing?"

"I want to see your muscles."

I snag her glasses and place them back on the nightstand. "How about you feel them instead?"

"I can agree to those terms."

I place my wallet on the nightstand before shoving my jeans and underwear down my legs. My cock pops out and I wrap my hand around the base before squeezing as hard as I can. I need to calm down before I come too early.

I'm not coming until Ginny has and not until I'm buried deep inside her.

I stand at the end of the bed and tap her legs. "Spread these."

She stares at me for a long moment. I don't push her. I wait. This has to be her decision. I blow out a breath in relief when she spreads her legs wide.

"Thank you."

I glide my hands up her legs until I reach her core. I trace a finger down her seam and her eyes close as she moans. It's the sweetest sound in the world.

I fit my shoulders between her legs until my mouth is positioned right where I want it. I inhale and her honey scent fills my lungs.

I flick my tongue at her clit and she nearly flies off the bed. I chuckle as I wrap an arm around her waist to keep her in the position I want her in.

While my finger plays with her opening, my tongue circles her clit in a light tease. It doesn't take long before she grasps my hair and pushes me down. I chuckle as I dive in.

Going down on a woman is usually a thing I do to get her riled up. It's not an act I particularly enjoy. But with Ginny it's different. Everything is different with her. I could feast on her for days. Lapping up her honey while her fingernails dig into my skull.

I want to play with her, deny her an orgasm for hours, but I fear my cock will explode if I wait any longer. I plunge two fingers into her pussy and suck on her clit at the same time and she explodes.

"Dylan," she groans. Groaning's good, but I want her to shout my name.

I continue to plunge my fingers in and out of her until her orgasm wanes and she collapses on the bed.

I get to my knees and wait for her eyes to open before I withdraw my fingers from her pussy. I stare into her eyes as I lick her juices from my fingers. Her eyes flare.

My little librarian isn't a prude in bed. It wouldn't matter if she was. I'd be glad to help her find her passion.

"Are you okay with more?"

"You did promise to show me your technique with your dick."

"No, I didn't."

Her brow wrinkles. "Yes, you did."

I cover her with my body. "I believe I used the word cock."

She blushes. The color travels from her checks down her long, elegant neck to the tops of her breasts. It's sexy as hell. I plan to make her blush while we're in bed as often as I can.

I reach for my wallet and remove a condom. I quickly don it before hitching my cock at her opening.

"Still okay with this?"

In response, she wraps her legs around my waist and squeezes. "I need to rate your technique."

I don't ask again. She's obviously on board.

I sink into her slowly. Enjoying the feel of her walls contracting against my cock. I don't stop until my balls slap her ass.

She moans and I grit my teeth before I come. I'm not a one-pump wonder. Not even when we first became famous and

I sampled fans like candy was I a one-pump wonder. And I am damn well not going to be one when I'm with the woman I'm falling for.

I bury my face in her shoulder and inhale her scent before getting to my knees and throwing her legs over my shoulders.

"This okay?"

Her inner walls squeeze me. "What do you think?"

I begin to glide in and out of her. I can't resist her breasts when they jiggle. I knead and massage them with my hands as I dip in and out of her pussy. She arches her back to thrust her chest closer to me and I pluck at her nipples.

Each time I pinch a nipple, her walls spasm around me. I wonder how far I can push it. I twist her nipple as I pinch it hard and her eyes fly open.

"I'm … I'm…" She doesn't finish her sentence before her walls strangle me and she moans with her orgasm.

Time to let go. I increase my pace until I'm pounding in and out of her. My lower back tingles and my balls heat as my orgasm barrels toward me.

"Yes, yes, yes," I chant as my rhythm fails me.

My climax hits. "Ginny," I growl as I ride out the euphoria.

My orgasm lasts forever. I continue to thrust until I've squeezed every last drop of pleasure from my body.

Holy shit. Virginia Hale rocked my world.

I was already falling for my little librarian but now I'm obsessed with spending as much time as I can in bed with her. I worried she'd be shy in bed, but she's my equal.

I think she might be my everything.

Chapter 22

VIRGINIA

I groan as I wake up. I stretch my arms in the air and muscles I forgot existed remind me of all the 'exercise' I got last night.

I thought after the first time, Dylan would roll away from me and fall asleep the way every other man I've ever had sex with before has.

Dylan is NOT the same as any other man I've known intimately. He has stamina and technique and no man will ever be good enough again. One night with him and he's ruined me for other men.

I'm not surprised. There's a reason I've been obsessed with the man since high school after all.

I roll over with a smile on my face but scowl when I realize Dylan isn't laying next to me. Did he sneak out on me? What a jerk! Who does he think he is? Having sex with me all night before—

I smell bacon. And coffee.

Maybe Dylan didn't desert me after all. Maybe I'm a nutcase who's worried she doesn't stack up against the other women he's been with.

He's a freaking rockstar. He can sleep with any woman in the world. What is he doing with me?

Unless he's only with me because he's in Winter Falls temporarily. Because there are no other available women my age. Because he's bored. Because he—

"Oh good. You're awake," Dylan says as he walks in carrying a tray.

My mouth gapes open. "You brought me breakfast in bed?"

His cheeks darken slightly. Oh my gosh. He is adorable when he's embarrassed.

"What did you bring me?" I ask since I never want him to be embarrassed.

"Pancakes."

I groan. "I love the pancakes from *Bake Me Happy*."

He growls. "I did not pick you up pancakes. I made pancakes."

"You made pancakes? You? The rockstar who can snap his fingers and get whatever and whoever he wants? Made *me* pancakes?"

He places the tray on my bedside table before sitting next to me on the bed and grasping my hands. "I only want you, Ginny. Not some faceless fan. Or aggressive groupie. You." He squeezes my hands. "Do you understand?"

I open my mouth to reassure him. To say all is well, end this conversation, and move on. But I'm not that person anymore.

I'm not the people pleaser who says whatever's necessary to stop her family or other students from bullying her.

I snap my mouth shut. I am Virginia Hale, librarian of Winter Falls, and an adult who has the right to ask questions. I can do this.

"Do you want me to get the fire extinguisher?" Dylan asks.

My brow wrinkles. "The fire extinguisher?"

"There's a whole lot of smoke coming out of your ears."

I roll my eyes. "Have a lot of experience with fire extinguishers, do you?"

He sighs. "Two words. Jett and Gibson."

"Does Fender never get in any trouble?"

He releases my hands to pinch my chin. "I'm happy to spend the morning telling you stories about my bandmates but first I want to know you understand I want you and not any other woman."

I blow out a breath. "It's kind of hard to believe. You're you and I'm me."

His gaze rakes up and down my body. "And what a sexy little one you are."

I squirm. "I'm not little."

"You're a foot shorter than me."

"I wasn't referring to my height."

He cocks an eyebrow. "You weren't?"

I slap his shoulder and he captures my hand to place it against his chest. "Ginny, I think I proved to you I love each and every one of your curves last night." He pauses to lean closer to me until I can feel his heat surrounding me. "But I'm happy to prove to you how much I enjoy those curves again this morning."

Heat flows through me until liquid pools between my thighs. I rub them together.

"You did promise to show me all of your techniques."

"Is there a technique you think needs improvement?"

I can feel my blush travel from my cheeks down my body to my chest, but I plow forward. "You didn't actually show me your … um… finger technique."

By the time I finish the sentence, my face is on fire.

Dylan smirks. "I didn't? I need to rectify this omission immediately."

His finger trails from my neck down my torso, around my breast, until he reaches the waistband of my panties. Why, oh why, did I insist on putting on a t-shirt to sleep in? If my chest was bare, I have no doubt his hands would be filled with my breasts.

He bends forward and places his mouth on my ear. "But first. Breakfast."

Breakfast? How can he possibly be thinking about food now?

"You're a tease," I grumble.

"I did promise to withhold at least one orgasm." I frown and he pinches my nose. "Plus, the pancakes are getting cold."

My stomach grumbles and he chuckles. "Let's feed the hungry beast, shall we?"

I rearrange the pillows behind me until I'm comfortable and he sets the tray on my lap. I inhale a deep breath of pancakes, maple syrup, and warm butter. Yum.

"These smell delicious. Where did you learn to cook?"

He settles next to me in bed. "I didn't have much choice after my dad left. My mom was working all the time. Someone had to feed my sisters breakfast."

"If I remember correctly, you were working all the time, too."

He shrugs and grabs one of the plates from the tray. "Mom was heartbroken. She needed time to grieve."

"Your sisters are lucky to have you."

I would have loved a sister growing up. Anything would have been better than the two step-brothers I ended up with.

I shove those thoughts away. I am not thinking about my so-called family when Dylan is sitting next to me in bed eating pancakes he made me as a treat after a night of lovemaking.

"I didn't feed Harry since it's morning but I removed all his uneaten food and gave him fresh water."

"You did what?"

He frowns. "Did I overstep? I'm sorry. You were sleeping and I didn't want to wake you. I won't do it again if it bothers you."

I capture his wrist. "It doesn't bother me."

"It doesn't?"

His voice sounds full of hope. As if he's the one who can't believe I'm with him instead of the other way around. Crazy but true.

"Of course not. Harry likes you. I have no idea why, but he does," I tease.

"No idea why?"

"Yeah. What's so special about you anyway?"

"What's special about me?"

"Yes, you're a rockstar who can make pancakes but there's probably tons of those in the world."

"Tons of those, huh?"

I shrug. I hope it appears nonchalant and not as if I don't know how to carry on teasing him.

He drops his plate on the nightstand with a clink before shoving the tray off my lap. It clatters to the floor.

Before I have a chance to tell him he is cleaning up his mess he crawls on top of me and pins me to the bed.

"Someone needs a reminder of how good I can make her feel."

His deep voice causes shivers to run through my body. Heat follows in their wake.

"A reminder might be necessary." I try to sound all prim and proper the way a librarian should but I don't think I achieve my goal. Not when my voice is all breathy and my chest is heaving.

Dylan presses his hard length into my stomach and I wrap my legs around his waist.

"Nope," he admonishes as he unwinds my legs. "I believe I have to demonstrate my finger technique first."

His hand trails down my side until he reaches my panties. He toys with the waistband until I'm squirming beneath him.

"When does this demonstration begin?" I ask when he doesn't continue his exploration past my waistband.

"Is someone impatient?"

I am but I will never admit it. Dylan will use the opportunity to slow things down.

"It's okay. I understand if you have performance anxiety."

He growls. "Performance anxiety?"

"Yeah, it's when you're worried your performance will not meet certain expectations."

"I know what performance anxiety is and I don't have it."

"Oh?" I push my glasses up my nose. "It appears as if you do."

His hand dives into my panties and he buries two fingers inside of me. I moan and my head falls back.

"Is this performance anxiety?" he asks as he thrusts his fingers in and out of me.

"What about this?" He withdraws his fingers to circle my clit before plunging his fingers into me once again.

As he continues to pump his fingers in me, he uses his free hand to lift my t-shirt until it's shoved up to my neck. He plucks and pinches at my nipples.

I'm in sensory overload. His hands are everywhere. Inside me, on me. I'm ready to explode and I'm still wearing my panties and t-shirt.

I plant my heels in the bed and use the leverage to move with his thrusts. My walls quiver around his fingers as I rush toward euphoria.

"Look at me," Dylan demands. My eyes fly open and I drop my chin to meet his gaze. "When you come all over my fingers, you look at me."

I should probably be embarrassed. The light is on and it's daytime, but I don't care. My body is in charge of this moment. No, Dylan is in charge of my body.

"Come, my little librarian. Come all over my fingers."

I gasp.

"And then you'll come all over my cock."

"I'm …" I don't finish the words before I'm falling off the cliff into oblivion.

I stare into Dylan's eyes as ecstasy flows through me. His eyes are on fire. He's not smug or arrogant. He's just Dylan. Happy to give me pleasure.

Maybe I shouldn't be so worried about his rockstar status. Maybe I should go with the flow. Enjoy what we have for as long as we have it.

Chapter 23

Liquid courage – come for the courage, stay for the laughs

DYLAN

"You okay with this?" I ask when we reach the *Naked Falls Brewery* to meet up with the band for dinner.

"Why wouldn't I be okay? Should I not be okay?" Ginny's words are sassy but pushing her glasses up her nose tells me she's not feeling as sassy as she's pretending to be.

Damn. I'm an idiot. I shouldn't have asked her if she's okay. Stupid question.

"My bandmates are idiots ninety-nine percent of the time," I say instead of backpedaling and reminding her of how shy and introverted she is.

"Indigo will be there." She will. "And rumor has it the food here is amazing."

"You haven't eaten here yet?" The brewery is one of only two places to eat out in town.

"Going out to eat often isn't in my budget." She smiles up at me. "Today's a treat."

"Today's also on me."

She scowls. "I don't need you to pay for me just because you're some big famous rockstar."

"I'm not paying for you because I'm a 'big famous rockstar'. I'm paying because you're my girlfriend, this is a date, and my mom would skin me alive if I didn't pay for you."

Everything I said is true, but what I don't say is how I'm not paying because I want her to save her money to buy the house she's dreaming of. I want all of her dreams to come true. And, hopefully, some of those future dreams will include me.

"Your mom sounds awesome." Her voice is wistful. I know she doesn't have a great relationship with her family, but she hasn't shared the details. Yet. In the meantime, I'm happy to share my family with her.

"Mom's going to love you when you meet."

"When we meet?" she squeaks.

"You're my girlfriend. It's normal for you to meet my family. I don't know if she'll wait for Christmas, though."

"Christmas?"

"Santa, list of who's naughty and nice, elves making presents for the nice children. Any of this ring a bell?"

She rolls her eyes. "I know what Christmas is."

She does, but she's no longer thinking about how nervous she is to meet my family. There's no reason to be nervous. I wasn't lying when I said my mom was going to love her. What's not to love?

Besides, Virginia is the first woman I plan to introduce to my mom and sisters. They're going to lose their minds. In a good way. It'll be loud – very, very loud – but good.

Her nose wrinkles. "I don't have much contact with my family."

Ah, she's not worried about meeting my mom and four sisters. She's worried I'll want to meet her family. And I do. But I can wait.

"I guess we're doing the holidays with my family then. Mom is going to love that. She hates it when Janis spends time with her in-laws."

"Did you forget Christmas is more than six months away?"

"I do have a calendar. Actually, I don't, but my watch has the date on it. Do you want to see?" I hold out my wrist to her.

She giggles as she bats me away. "What about appointments? Don't you have an agenda on your phone?"

I make a face. "The band's assistant, Aurora, is always sending us calendar updates and appointments. I prefer it when she just tells us where and when to show up. I don't need the details."

"Don't you want to plan in advance?"

"What's there to plan?"

"What to wear? What to say? A thousand strategies for escaping should the need arise."

I bark out a laugh. "If I want to escape, I get up and walk out. And I say whatever I want."

"You say whatever you want? Aren't you supposed to be all – I don't know – prepped by public relations or something?"

"Our manager sent us to some PR-conscious seminar crap when we first hit it big. It lasted three days until Gibson seduced one of the women and Jett disappeared with one of the men to go base jumping."

Her eyes widen. "Base jumping? Isn't that dangerous?"

"Dangerous is Jett's middle name."

I notice Gibson, Jett, and Fender strolling our way and wave.

"Are you going to stand out here all night making out with your girlfriend or are we going inside?" Jett asks.

"Dude, they're not making out, or have you forgotten how two people have to be touching lips for it to be considered making out?" Gibson asks. "Do you need some pointers? I'm always willing to help."

Jett shoves Gibson. "I don't need any pointers from you. Did you forget I'm winning?"

"What is he winning?" Ginny whispers her question.

I don't answer. I'm not telling her how two of my bandmates have an ongoing competition about how many women they can have sex with. She's having a hard enough time handling how I'm a musician. Their bet would throw her over the edge.

I step between Jett and Gibson. "Knock it off, numbskulls. If you get banned from the brewery, you won't have anywhere else to eat in town."

Not to mention, if they get banned, the rest of the band will be as well. Considering I plan to spend a lot of time in Winter Falls in the future, I want to be able to eat here.

Jett sticks his thumbs in his belt loops and saunters to the door. "They wouldn't ban us. We're practically family." Fender and Gibson follow him.

"Family?" Ginny asks.

"Two of Cash's half-brothers own the place."

"Maybe I should join the town Facebook group," she mumbles as I lead her inside.

"The town Facebook group?"

She doesn't have a chance to answer before Indigo shouts, "Virginia!" and jumps to greet her as if they haven't seen each other in ages.

I raise an eyebrow at Cash.

"Someone needed a bit of liquid courage for her first performance review."

Indigo releases Ginny to turn on Cash. "I did not need liquid courage. The principal, Mrs. West, and I had a drink to celebrate what a wonderful school year it's been."

"One drink?"

"What's the difference between one or two drinks?" Indigo's nose wrinkles. "Or was it three?"

Jett snorts. "And here everyone thought Gibson and I would be the reason we get banned from the brewery."

A waitress arrives. "Your table is ready."

We follow her upstairs to a table tucked away in the corner. I pull a chair out for Ginny before sitting next to her.

"Ah, he pulled the chair out for her." Gibson bats his eyelashes. "It must be love."

It's not love yet but I'm traveling down the road toward my final destination marked as love.

Jett shakes his head. "Love isn't pulling out a chair. Love is swallowing." He leans toward Ginny but I slap a hand over his mouth before he can question her.

"Stop being rude."

Jett gasps. "I'm not rude. I'm exciting and new. I'm life's sweetest reward."

Ginny giggles. "Are you paraphrasing the Love Boat theme?"

"I'm making it better."

"The judges of the karaoke contest beg to differ," Gibson claims.

Jett sniffs and sticks his nose in the air. "I can't understand why I didn't win."

Fender grunts. "Cash was there."

"Did Fender just give you a compliment?" Indigo probably thinks she's whispering to Cash but she's not. She's shouting.

"How many drinks did you have with the principal anyway?" Ginny asks.

Indigo counts on her fingers. "One. Two. Three. No. Two. Definitely two."

Ginny sighs. "You never could count." She glances around the table and whisper-shouts, "She used to cheat off me all the time."

"I did not!"

Ginny raises an eyebrow at Indigo. "You just happened to drop your pencil next to my desk every five minutes during every single test in math class our sophomore year?"

Indigo crosses her arms over her chest. "It was rude of you to skip a year."

"I'm the rude one?" She points to herself. "I bet you ten bucks Dylan can tell a story about everyone at this table which proves they're ruder than me."

I rub my hands together. "I'm ready."

Indigo glares at Ginny. "Make it twenty."

"You got it." They shake hands before Ginny motions to me. "Please proceed."

"This is too easy. Jett and Gibson are the definition of rude."

"Talk. Talk. Talk." Indigo crosses her arms over her chest. "You're not proving anything."

"Let's see. How about the time Gibson woke up in a hotel room with some woman. He returned from the bathroom to discover her snuggling up in bed. He pulled the sheets off the bed and threw her clothes at her before pointing at the door. Which is all pretty normal Gibson behavior but then his phone rang and he put it on speaker and arranged a date for that night while his date from the previous evening was standing there getting dressed."

Gibson taps his forehead. "I still have the scar from where she threw the remote control at my head."

Jett studies the scar. "She had awesome aim. Was she a softball pitcher?"

Gibson shrugs. "I don't ask what they do for a living."

Indigo moans. "No fair. I forgot we're sitting with a rock band."

"You forgot your boyfriend is the lead singer of a rock band?" Ginny giggles. "Maybe we should cut you off."

"But I want to try a beer from Cash's brothers' brewery."

"You don't drink beer."

I watch Indigo and Virginia argue and release the breath I'd been holding. I'll never admit it out loud but I was worried about

Ginny hanging around the band this evening. Not only is she shy and introverted but she isn't exactly comfortable with my fame.

But there was nothing to worry about. Her shyness disappears when she's around people she's comfortable with. And it gives me great pleasure to note she's comfortable around my bandmates.

Good. Because she's going to be spending a whole lot of time with them in the future.

Chapter 24

Surprise – a surefire way to get your girl to cry

VIRGINIA

I settle on the sofa and open my book. It's Saturday afternoon and the library is closed. It's the perfect time to catch up on some reading.

I scowl when there's a knock on the door. I haven't even read the first page yet. I grunt and go to answer it. I check the peephole and notice it's Dylan.

"What are you doing here?" I ask when I open the door.

He chuckles before brushing his lips against mine. "Is that how you greet your boyfriend?"

I have to admit his greeting is way better than mine.

"I didn't expect you. I thought you were in the studio today."

"We're nearly finished recording now. We just needed to polish up one of the songs."

My heart clamors against my chest. They're nearly finished? Will he leave Winter Falls once they are? When will I see him again? Will I see him again?

"I've got a surprise for you."

At the word 'surprise' all my worries about the future and Dylan disappear. I love surprises.

"What is it?"

He rolls his eyes. "It wouldn't be a surprise if I told you, would it?"

I scan the hallway. "Where is it?"

He chuckles. "Get your shoes on and I'll show you."

I place my book on the side table in the hallway – being in a hurry is no excuse to throw a book – and slip my feet into a pair of flip-flops.

"Real shoes. Not sandals."

"I need real shoes for this surprise?" What could it be? What requires real shoes? "Are we going out?"

"In a manner of speaking." I glare at him. "What?"

"You're being deliberately vague."

"It wouldn't be a surprise if I gave it away."

Darn it. He's right. I pick up a pair of tennis shoes. "These okay?"

"Yep."

Tennis shoes are okay, I muse as I put them on. We're obviously not going to a fancy restaurant. Where could we possibly be going?

"Do I need my purse?" I ask once I'm wearing the appropriate footwear.

"Nope."

Dylan grasps my hand and leads me out of my apartment and down the stairs. "May I cover your eyes?"

I bounce up and down. This is so fun! "Yes."

"Here we go." He holds a hand in front of my eyes and steers me outside. We don't walk far. Maybe a few feet before we stop. "You ready?"

"Yes. A thousand times yes."

He chuckles as he removes his hands. "Ta-da!"

There are two bikes standing next to one another. One is pink with tassels on the handlebars and a white basket up front. It's cute and exactly what I wanted for my sixteenth birthday.

My eyes itch and I sniff. Dylan pulls me into his arms. "Do you not like it? I can return it. No big deal."

"You are not returning my bike!" I shout loud enough for the entire state of Colorado to hear. "How did you know?"

"I asked Indigo."

"You're cheating but I'll allow it this one time because I have a pretty pink bike."

"How am I cheating?"

"You just are," I declare before rushing to the bike – *my* bike. I run my hand along the frame.

"You like it?"

"I don't like it. I love it! Thank you!" I throw myself at Dylan. I don't worry about him catching me. I trust him. He'll always catch me.

I trust Dylan? When did this happen? Nope. I'm not worrying about it. Not today.

Dylan holds me tight. I usually enjoy his arms around me but I squirm to get away. I want to try out my new bike.

"Let's go for a ride."

I don't wait for his response before jumping on my bike and pedaling around the parking lot. I'm a little unsteady at first. It's been years since I rode a bike. But I quickly get the hang of it.

"Come on, slow poke," I yell at Dylan when he merely stands there.

He climbs onto the other bike and together we bike out of the parking lot.

"Where should we go?" I ask.

"I have a route planned."

I break to a stop. "You have a route planned?"

He nods. "And a picnic."

"You have a route and a picnic planned?"

"I can't exactly give you a bike without a plan."

"Did I say thank you yet?"

He grins. "You did."

"Oh, okay. I guess I won't thank you later tonight then."

He swallows. "You can always thank me again."

I shrug. "Maybe."

"You haven't seen the picnic yet. When you see the picnic, you'll change your mind."

"Where is this picnic?" I throw my arms out. "I don't see any picnic."

"Come on." He starts pedaling. "I'll show you."

I hurry to catch up to him. "Where are we going?"

Dylan chuckles at my impatience. "It's a surprise."

I huff. "I already got the bike as a surprise. You can tell me."

"And here I thought you were patient."

"I am patient."

"Except when it comes to surprises," he mumbles as we turn onto a biking trail toward the river.

"I don't get many surprises. So, sue me for getting overexcited."

"Things are changing, my little librarian. From now on, you'll be getting more surprises than you know what to do with."

"Promises. Promises. Pro…"

My words trail off when we round a bend and the river and falls come into view. "Wow."

It's beautiful here. The mountains are in the background, far away, and nearby is flowing water with lush green surrounding it.

"Let's stop here," Dylan suggests but I'm already slowing down.

We dismount our bikes and he leads us toward the waterfall.

"This is the waterfall for which Winter Falls is named," he tells me.

"How do you know?"

"I may have done a bit of research for today's outing."

"You keep surprising me."

He winks. "That's the idea."

We walk a bit further until we reach a meadow overlooking the waterfall and river. "We can leave our bikes here."

We park our bikes and he grasps my hand. "Ready?"

I bounce on my toes. "Ready!"

He whirls me around and points to the middle of the clearing where there's a checkered picnic blanket with a wicker picnic basket on top of it. I hurry toward it.

"I've never had a picnic before," I say as he helps me onto the blanket.

"Never?"

"Nope."

"Not even when you were a kid?"

"Do I need to explain the definition of never to you?"

"Smart ass."

"Have you had many picnics before?" I ask and immediately regret it. I don't need the details of the other romantic encounters he's had. I know he's had them. Details are not needed.

"When one of my sisters was having a bad day, I'd make her favorite food and we'd have a picnic on the living room floor while watching her favorite movie."

I sigh. "You're the best brother ever."

Unlike my a-word step-brothers who thought it was fun to torture me more when I was having a bad day. I learned awful quick to hide my emotions from them.

He snorts. "They didn't think I was the best brother ever when I reminded them to finish their homework or grilled their dates."

But he cared and they knew it. I bet they think he's the best brother now.

He opens the picnic basket. "What do we have here?"

"I don't know." I peer inside. "Holy cow. Did you make all of this?"

"It wasn't hard," he claims as he begins to remove containers from the basket, but his blush tells a different story.

I kiss his cheek. "Thank you."

"You're welcome, Ginny."

I have the feeling he has more to say but he returns his attention to the basket and pulls out a bottle of champagne.

"I know you prefer beer but I thought you might want to try this."

I snatch the bottle from him. "Try this? Of course, I want to try this. I've never had champagne before."

"You've never had champagne before?"

I roll my eyes. "Not all of us are famous rockstars."

"If you enjoy it, we'll drink it more often."

He takes the bottle from me and opens it. I squeal and clap when it pops. I dig some glasses out of the basket and he fills them.

"To us." I hold up my glass.

"To us," he repeats and clinks my glass with his.

I sip my drink and giggle when the bubbles tickle my nose.

"Do you like it?"

"It's fruity and bubbly and yummy."

He grins. "Good."

My stomach rumbles and he chuckles. "I guess I better feed you."

"I think I forgot to eat lunch," I mutter. I didn't forget to eat lunch. I skipped lunch and planned to have an early dinner. But I'm not reminding Mr. Money Bags about my economical lifestyle.

He fixes me a plate of potato salad, coleslaw, and fried chicken. "It smells delicious," I say as I dig in. I groan. The potato salad is perfect. Not too much mayo. The way I prefer it.

He makes his own plate and we sit side by side gazing at the waterfall as we eat.

"What time do you need to return your bike?" I ask once I finish my food.

"Why would I need to return my bike?"

"You rented it for the entire weekend?"

"It's not a rental. I bought it."

I scrunch my nose. "But you won't be in Winter Falls much longer."

He grasps my chin and forces me to face him. "You're here, Ginny. I'll be in Winter Falls as often and as much as I can as long as you're here."

Hope starts to build in my chest. "You will?"

"Of course."

Hope bursts throughout me. Dylan isn't fleeing Winter Falls as soon as he can. He won't abandon me once the album is finished.

Maybe the Virginia and Dylan story won't be a short one after all.

Chapter 25

VIRGINIA

"Good job."

My mouth gapes open. Did Gratitude seriously tell me I did a good job at something? Miracles do happen!

"Thank you," I murmur once I remember how to form words.

"This is the kind of work I expect from you when I retire."

I clench my jaw before my mouth can gape open again. This is the first time the r-word has left her lips since I arrived in Winter Falls in January. I was beginning to think she forgot all about the whole retirement thing.

"I'm taking the rest of the day off. I expect things to be shipshape when I open the library tomorrow morning."

"Of course. Have a nice afternoon."

I hold my tongue as she gathers her things and walks out the front door. Once she's no longer visible, I squeal. "Yes!"

A woman reading a book on a comfy chair in the corner scowls at me and I mouth *sorry*.

I hum as I finish entering the new books into the computer system. The afternoon passes quickly. Students arrive after school finishes to study and liven the place up. Although the woman reading in the corner glares at them.

Once closing time arrives, I usher the students out and lock the front door. I hurry down the hallway to the office to grab my purse. I can't wait to tell Dylan how Gratitude is trusting me more. I'd nearly given up hope of her actually retiring in my lifetime.

I open the office door but don't bother to switch on the lights. I reach for my purse but stop when I hear a knock. I listen. There it is again.

The sound didn't come from the front of the library. It was closer by. Maybe the window? Is someone knocking on the window?

My heart races as I inch toward the window. I think it's shut and locked but I need to make sure before I leave for the night.

Someone mumbles before the window flips open and a person flies through it.

"Aaaah!" I scream. I drop my purse and run from the room to the main area of the library where I crouch behind the circulation desk.

I grab the phone from the desk and it clatters to the floor. I freeze as I wait for the intruder to find me. When no one comes rushing at me, I phone Dylan. I need three tries before my shaking fingers finally dial the correct number.

"Hey, Ginny. Are you almost finished for the day? It's lovely weather so I was thinking we could maybe grill."

"Intruder," I gasp.

"Intruder?"

"There's someone in the library."

"Get out of there. Get out right now!"

"I can't. The library is my responsibility."

"It's not the fucking Alamo. Get out of there."

A door squeaks open. "He's coming closer," I whisper.

"Hide. Make yourself as small as possible. I'll be there in three minutes."

"Don't hang up."

"I won't but I need to put you on speaker while I bike."

"Okay."

"Are you hidden?" He's out of breath. He must be cycling toward me already.

I crawl under the desk and curl into a ball in the darkest corner. "Yes."

"Good. I'm coming Ginny. I won't let anything happen to you."

"I know." Dylan will handle this. He won't let me be hurt.

Books clash to the floor and I slam a hand over my mouth to hide my gasp. The intruder is getting closer.

Do they know I'm here? Will they search for me? What are they doing here? We don't have anything worth stealing in the library. Anyone in town can borrow as many books as they want at one time. And the computers are older than me.

"Ginny!" The doors rattle as Dylan pounds on them, but I don't dare move to unlock them. I'm frozen here under the desk.

I wrap my arms around my legs and sway back and forth. Back and forth.

The front door bursts open. I squeeze my eyes shut. I can't look. I can't look.

"Halt!" someone shouts before shoes pound on the floor. There's shuffling with some grunting.

I'm such a wimp. I should be out there helping. Instead, I'm stuck under my desk like a big fat scaredy-cat.

Wimp! Scaredy-cat! Coward! Sissy!

I cover my ears with my hands but the words don't stop.

"Ginny."

"No! No!"

A hand lands on my shoulder and I scream as long and as hard as I can. "STOOOOOOP!"

"Ginny! Ginny! Ginny!"

Wait. My step-brothers don't call me Ginny. To them, I'm 'Virginia the forever virgin'.

I slowly open my eyes. Dylan is kneeling in front of me with his hands up, palms out.

"It's me, Ginny. Dylan."

I fly at him and tackle him to the floor.

"Thank you for coming," I manage to say before I burst into tears.

He wraps his arms around me and holds me close. "You're okay, Ginny. You're okay. No one's going to hurt you."

When my tears slow, he lifts my head and wipes the moisture from my face. "Feeling better?" I nod. "Ready to sit up?"

I realize we're laying on the floor at my place of work. I struggle to sit up and end up kneeing him in the crotch.

"Ow!" he yelps.

"Sorry. Sorry. Sorry." I scramble to my feet.

I nearly crawl under the desk again when I realize the library is no longer empty. The chief of police is standing in the middle of the room with his hands on his hips while Indigo and the rest of Dylan's band surround him.

"What is everyone doing here?" And could this be any more embarrassing? At least the heat emitting from my face could power the library for the rest of the year.

"Enjoying my last minutes of freedom before the police haul me off to prison for murder," Indigo says.

"Um. What?" I scan the area. "Is someone dead? What are you talking about?"

She growls and points at Jett. "I'm going to kill him."

She launches herself at him but Cash wraps an arm around her waist to stop her. "It's probably best not to announce you're going to kill someone in front of the chief of police."

The chief ambles toward me. "Virginia, I'm Lyric, the chief of police."

Dylan wraps an arm around me and hauls me close. I'm surprised he doesn't grunt the word *mine*. I pat his stomach.

"I'm okay now," I lie. I'm not okay now. But I will be. Especially if Dylan keeps me wrapped up close.

"I'm not," he growls.

"Why? What's wrong?"

He points to Jett. "I'm going to kill him."

"We can make it a group effort. It'll be one of those bonding experiences Aurora's always begging us to try," Cash says.

Gibson raises his hand. "I'm in."

Fender crosses his arms over his chest and grunts.

Lyric clears his throat. "I'd really appreciate it if you'd stop discussing murder in front of me."

"Especially my murder," Jett adds and everyone glares at him. Why is everyone glaring at him? What am I missing?

"Where's the intruder?" I ask.

"You're looking at him." Indigo motions to Jett.

My brow wrinkles. "You're saying Jett broke into the library?"

Jett drops his chin to his chest. "I did."

I must be hearing things. "You broke into the library?"

"Yes."

"You crawled through the window of my office and scared me to death on purpose?"

At his nod, I lose it.

"What is wrong with you? I was terrified. I thought I was going to die. I thought I'd never see Dylan again." Tears flow down my cheeks but I'm not finished. "Do you have any idea how it feels to be scared so bad you can't breathe? To realize you have nowhere to go and no one is going to save you? Do you? Do you???"

Dylan buries my face in his shoulder and I cling to him.

"Ginny, you're safe. I promise you're safe. You'll always be safe as long as I'm around."

I believe him. I'm safe with him. It's why I love him.

I'm not startled by the revelation. It was bound to happen after all. Dylan's shown me I can depend on him, and I can trust him. And then there's the whole sexy thing and nights spent in his arms. Of course, I love him.

I gaze up at him. "Thank you."

He smiles. "You never need to thank me."

Lyric clears his throat and I glance over at him. "I think someone could do with a night in jail." He twirls his cuffs as he approaches Jett who holds up his hands as he backs away.

"It was a prank."

"A prank?" No way. No way did Jett scare me for a prank. He's not an a-word. Or, at least, I thought he wasn't. "What kind of prank?"

"Um…" Jett bites his lip.

"It doesn't matter," Dylan grumbles. "He should have known better."

"I am sorry, Virginia," Jett says but I have no response. It was a prank? A prank?!

Lyric grasps his shoulder and whirls him around before snatching his hand and snapping the handcuffs in place.

"Let's go." The chief of police leads Dylan's bandmate out of the library. This is a nightmare. Only I'm not sleeping.

Fender's the first person to move. He stops in front of me. "Jett's an idiot. I'm sorry he scared you."

"It wasn't your fault."

"Let me know if you need anything," he says to Dylan before leaving.

Gibson's next. "He didn't mean to scare you."

Dylan growls behind me. "He should have known better."

"True." Gibson clears his throat. "I'm around if you need anything."

Indigo waits until Fender and Gibson are gone to throw herself at me. "Jett is such an idiot. I'm so sorry. In his defense, he doesn't know about your past. It doesn't make what he did okay and I will be delivering some brownies laced with Ex-lax to his jail cell tonight, but he didn't know."

She squeezes me one more time before releasing me. I know what her squeeze means. She thinks I should tell Dylan about my past. As if I have a choice after today.

Cash kisses my cheek. "I'm glad you're okay, Virginia."

Once they're gone, I'm left alone with Dylan. He draws a hand down his face. "Fuck. You scared me today."

"It wasn't my intention."

"I'm not blaming you. Sorry if it sounded as if I were."

I inhale a deep breath and blow it out. Getting defensive with the man who came to my rescue was not my intention either.

"I'm ready to go home."

"I'm just going to check all the windows and doors are locked," Dylan says and stalks off.

He's making sure I feel safe. Again. How can I not love this man?

Shit. I have to tell him about my past.

Chapter 26

VIRGINIA

"What do you want for dinner?" Dylan asks when we enter my apartment.

He's ready to move on from what happened in the library but I can't. If I don't tell him why I had a complete meltdown now, I won't ever tell him.

I hate telling people about my past. Despite Indigo being my closest friend in high school, I would have *never* told her what happened if I hadn't had a panic attack during a field trip to the zoo in our junior year.

"Can we talk?"

"Do I need an adult beverage for this talk?" He jokes but there's worry in his eyes.

"I think we both do."

"Sit." He kisses my forehead before grabbing two beers from the refrigerator. He hands one to me before joining me on the sofa. "Unless you think we need tequila for this conversation."

I pretend to ponder the idea.

"Shit. I'm not going to enjoy this, am I?"

"No."

"Promise you're not breaking up with me."

He's the one who will be doing the breaking up once he hears my pathetic story.

"I'm not breaking up with you."

"You didn't say you promise."

"I promise I'm not breaking up with you."

He blows out a breath. "Thank fuck."

His relief causes a tiny bit of hope to awaken inside of me. Not quite a spark, but it's there. I sip on my beer and ponder where to begin. Have I mentioned how much I hate discussing my past?

Dylan squeezes my hand. "You don't have to tell me anything you're not ready to tell me. I can wait. I'm a patient man."

I want to latch onto the out he's giving me but I won't. I love this man. He needs to know the truth about my past – whether I want him to or not.

I blow out a breath. "I need to tell you why I freaked out at the library."

"Because Jett's an idiot who broke in through the window of your office and scared the hell out of you."

"You're kind. My reaction was over the top and you know it."

He shrugs. "You have a right to react how you need to react to whatever situation."

"You always know the right thing to say." I never stood a chance of keeping my heart closed off from him.

He snorts. "Try convincing my sister Stevie of that. When she had her very first period and I was the only person home while she was freaking out, she didn't appreciate me telling her to calm down it's only a period."

"Poor Stevie," I murmur.

Dylan groans. "You're going to gang up on me with my sisters and mom, aren't you?"

I hope I get the chance to meet his mom and sisters. But once he learns about my past, he might not want to have anything to do with me anymore.

I need to get this over with. I need to get the words out and stop worrying about the what-ifs in the future.

I swallow. "I told you my dad died when I was young."

"I'm sorry."

"I don't really remember him. Mom married my step-dad, Terrance, when I was four." I wish I didn't remember my step-dad. "They had two kids. Two sons – Edward and Aaron."

I pause. Now comes the hard part.

"My step-dad never liked me. It was perfectly clear I wasn't *his* child with the way he treated me differently than Edward and Aaron. I'd come home with As in school and he'd ask why one grade was an A-. Why didn't I put in more effort? Meanwhile, Edward and Aaron were praised for getting Cs. They got Playstations and gift certificates for their 'academic achievements'. I got nothing."

Dylan growls. "Asshole."

"Terrance criticized everything I did. I didn't wash the dishes right. I didn't set the table right. I didn't bring him his beer fast enough. I learned to be quiet and hide in my room as often as I could."

"You didn't feel safe."

"At the start, I felt safe enough. I became the mouse Terrance thought I was."

He growls. "You are not a mouse."

I was, though. But not anymore. At least, not most of the time.

"Once Edward and Aaron were older, things got worse." I steel myself for his reaction to this next bit. "They were constantly invading my room. They'd do all sorts of pranks. Put spiders or dead mice in my room, steal my homework. You get the idea."

"They tormented you."

"I handled it."

He squeezes my hand. "What did your mom say?"

"Boys will be boys."

"What a cop out."

Relief courses through me at his words. He gets it. He understands.

"Even when they brought the snake to my room and kept shoving it into my face and I was screaming in terror, her response didn't change."

Dylan pulls me into his arms. "I don't need to hear any more. I've heard enough. Your family is a bunch of assholes."

I cringe. "I don't like to call them a-words."

He pinches my chin and lifts it until our eyes meet. His blue eyes are full of anger. "And I don't like knowing you were tormented as a child."

"I'm not weak."

"I never said you were."

"I sound weak."

"Is that why you didn't tell me this before?"

I consider lying but if I want Dylan and I have to have a chance at a future, he needs to know the truth. All of it.

"I thought you'd dump me if you knew the truth."

"Dump you? Why the hell would I dump you because your mom is weak, your step-dad is an asshole, and your step-brothers tormented you?"

"This is why I love you. No matter what I say you're on my side. It's …" I trail off when I realize he's staring at me with his mouth gaping open. "What's wrong? Do you want to dump me after all? I understand. I—"

My words are cut off when he melds his lips to mine. I gasp and he shoves his tongue into my mouth. His clean and fresh scent hits me and I sink into the kiss. I forget all about my family and my embarrassment about having a panic attack in front of the entire town.

All I can think about is him. Dylan. The man I love. The man who makes my entire body go up in flames.

I climb into his lap and cling to his shoulders as his tongue strokes against mine. As he explores every inch of my mouth. As if he can't get enough. As if he'll never get enough.

When he rips his mouth from mine, he's gasping for breath. "You love me?"

"What?" I do, but I didn't tell him. Did I?

"You can't take the words back now."

I rewind our conversation in my mind. I groan when I realize the 'I love you' slipped out.

"I know it's too soon. I promise I'm not a stage five clinger."

He chuckles. "It's not too soon and you can cling as much as you want. I want you to cling."

"You want me to cling? I'm confused. Men don't want clingy women." I've read enough romance novels to know this is true.

"I love you. I want you near me all the time. But I didn't say anything because I thought you'd run away if you knew how I feel about you."

My eyes are the size of saucers by the time he's finished. "You. Love. Me?"

He palms my neck and lays his forehead against mine. "I love you, Virginia Hale."

"Despite knowing what a wimp I was growing up and watching me have a panic attack over a prank?"

He squeezes my neck. "One, you aren't a wimp. You were tortured. Your mother should be ashamed of herself. In fact, what's your mother's name and address?"

"You aren't going to have her killed, are you?"

His grin is downright wicked. "Worse. I'll sic my mom on her."

"Oh my. I would pay to see their confrontation."

"No need to pay. Give me the information and it's done."

I gape at him. "You're serious?"

"As a broken guitar pick."

I shake my head. "I can't."

He ignores me. "And once my mom has shamed your mother, I'll sic Fender on your dad and brothers."

I raise an eyebrow. "Fender?"

"He makes grown men shit their pants with a look. And since I'm not allowed to have them killed, it's the best option."

"There's been an awful lot of talk about killing people today."

"It's been a busy day."

"My head is spinning. I can't keep up."

Dylan kisses my nose. "I'll catch you up. Your family are a bunch of assholes, which my mom is going to love. She won't have to share us during the holidays. Jett is a fucking idiot. As soon as he's out of jail, I'm kicking his ass. I love you. You love me. Any questions?"

"You love me?" I can't believe it. Maybe I'm in some kind of anxiety attack induced dream state.

"I love you." Those ocean blue eyes I've loved since I was a teenager are full of honesty for a moment before they sparkle with mischief. "But I could show you instead of telling you."

"Show me? How are you going to show me?"

He lifts his hips and I feel his hard length press against my core. I can play this game. In fact, I'm all in.

"I don't know." I tap my cheek. "I think I need a demonstration."

"Your wish is my command."

He stands with me in his arms.

"Holy cow, you're strong."

"And big." He winks.

Being carried by the man I love to the bedroom for him to show me some sexy times is not how I thought this day would end, but I'm on board with this plan. I'll even spring for a first-class ticket.

Chapter 27

Making love – not easy to do when a sexy minx tempts you until you lose your mind

DYLAN

We reach the bedroom and I lay Ginny down on the bed. My hands shake with nerves as I stare down at her. This isn't sex. And it sure as hell isn't fucking. This is making love. I need to prove to her I love her with all my being. That I don't care about her past. That she's it for me.

She pushes her glasses up her nose. "What's wrong?"

"Just trying to figure out where to start."

"I know where I want you to start."

I lift a brow.

"You can strip for me."

My cock jumps at the idea. He wants to strip for this woman. I know better. If I'm naked before her, I'll never last.

"Not a good idea."

"I'm sorry. I shouldn't have asked. I understand you have body confidence issues."

I growl. "Body confidence issues?"

"You know. You are uncomfortable in your body. Trust me. I get it. No judgment from me," she says with a little smirk on her face.

After the heavy talk in the living room, I didn't expect her to tease me. This woman is unbelievably strong, and I'm going to show her she's my everything.

"You think I have body issues?"

She shrugs. "No judgment. I love you anyway."

"You'd love me if I had a dad bod?"

"Yep. Because while your body is pretty spectacular." She rakes her gaze up and down me. "I love you for you. Because you're kind. Because you are always there for me when I need you. Because you understand me."

How can I resist stripping for her now? I can't.

I step away from the bed to give myself room, and she sits up. She fluffs the pillow behind her and settles in for the show. "I'm ready."

I kick my shoes off before digging my phone out of my back pocket. I scroll through the music until I find the song I want. *Blurred Lines* begins to play and Ginny cheers. And here I thought I'd need time to get my little librarian to open up in the bedroom.

I grab the hem of my t-shirt and draw it up my chest and over my head. I whirl it around in the air before throwing it toward Ginny. She catches it with a squeal.

I sway my hips to the music. Her eyes flare and she licks her lips. I whirl around and shake my ass at her and – smack!

I wag a finger at her. "No touching the dancer."

She sticks out her bottom lip in a pout. "But I want to."

I want to lick her lip before diving into her mouth, but if Ginny wants a show, she's getting a show.

"Respect the talent."

Her nose wrinkles. "Should the talent be talking?" She whirls her finger around. "Get to it, talent."

"No more touching," I order before starting to dance again.

I toy with my belt buckle and she licks her lips. My cock – already hard and ready to go – hardens further until it's almost painful. The good kind of pain I want to experience every day for the rest of my life. The kind of pain *I will* experience every day for the rest of my life with this woman. The woman I love who loves me. I'm one lucky bastard.

I unbuckle my belt and pull it out of the loops of my jeans. I whip it around a few times while swaying to the music before I let it drop to the floor.

When I unsnap my jeans and lower the zipper, Ginny licks her lips. My little librarian's eyes are focused on my cock as I shove my jeans and underwear to the floor.

Before I know what's happening, she's sitting on the edge of the bed with my hard length in her hand.

"Ginny," I groan as she squeezes me.

My head falls back as pleasure whips through my body at the feel of her soft hands on me. I nearly jump when she blows on my cock before her mouth engulfs me.

"My love," I growl. I force my eyes open to look down at her.

She bats her eyelashes at me but doesn't stop moving her mouth up and down my length.

"I won't last long, my love."

She pops off of me. "If you want me to stop, calling me your love is not helping things."

Before I have a chance to respond, her mouth is on me once again. It's hot and wet and Ginny. I want to tell her to stop. This isn't me showing her I love her. But this *is* Ginny showing me her love.

I thread my hands through her hair to pull it away from her face. I want to watch her going down on me. Watch her mouth swallow my cock while her hands play with my balls. I want to…

My lower back tingles and my balls tighten. Shit. I'm not coming in her mouth. Not today at least. I'll add it to my agenda for another day.

I use my hold on her hair to pull her off of me. "Enough."

"I wasn't finished."

"But I nearly was and I'm not finishing until I'm buried deep inside you."

She sighs. "I guess if you don't have enough stamina for two rounds."

I pick her up and throw her in the middle of the bed before laying on top of her. "Are you saying I don't have stamina?"

She giggles. "I think I was pretty clear."

"I'll show you stamina."

"Promises. Promises."

She thinks she can taunt me, does she? Not on my watch.

I get to my knees. "Someone's wearing entirely too many clothes."

She lifts her arms above her head thrusting those gorgeous breasts upwards. "Get to it, Mr. Stamina Man."

"Your wish is my command, my little librarian."

I undo the buttons of her blouse until it falls open to reveal her lacy white bra. I trace a finger along the edge of the lace. She locks her legs around my waist and begins to rub herself up and down my length.

"Nuh-uh, my love. You're not getting yourself off by grinding against me."

"Why not?" she pouts.

I can't resist pulling her bottom lip into my mouth and sucking. "Because," I say against her lips, "I said so."

"Who are you? The enforcer of all things sex in my bedroom?"

I chuckle. "I like this title."

She pinches my side. "I'm not referring to you as enforcer."

I wiggle my eyebrows. "I'll make it worth your while."

She reaches between us to squeeze my cock. "You're going to make it worth my while anyway."

She's not wrong. She's also not releasing my cock.

"If you don't stop squeezing me, I'm going to come all over your stomach," I grit out.

She releases me to wrap her arms around my shoulders. She uses her hold to pull herself up to whisper in my ear. "Next time."

I groan. "You little minx."

I bite her lip before getting to my knees. I enjoy the vision of her with her blouse hanging open and her breasts heaving for a moment before I unsnap her pants and pull the zipper down. My hand dives into her panties and I sink a finger into her.

"You're fucking soaked."

"Do I need to explain how biology works to you? How a woman's body prepares itself for sex?"

Her clinical words should be a turn-off. But apparently, this woman could say anything and I'd want to rip her panties off and fuck her until we're both satisfied. Which is exactly what I'm going to do.

I drag her pants down her legs and throw them behind me. She's now laid out before me in her bra and panties with her blouse still on. I should probably remove her blouse. I'm supposed to be making love to her and not pounding her into the mattress but my cock has no patience left.

I grasp the edge of her panties and pull until they rip open.

She gasps. "Did you seriously just rip my panties?"

"Yep."

"Caveman."

"Your caveman."

I nudge her legs open and settle my hips between her thighs. I notch my cock at her entrance. Ginny wraps her legs around my hips and I push inside.

Fuck. She's hot and wet and perfect. I—

"Shit. Shit. Shit."

"What's wrong?"

"Condom. I forgot a condom."

I withdraw, intent on finding a condom and returning to bury myself in her as soon as possible, but her thighs clamp down to stop me from moving.

"Do you love me?"

I meet her gaze and smile. "Yes, Virginia, I love you with all my heart."

"Then, there's no need for a condom."

"But I want to protect you. It's my job to protect you."

Her smile widens and lights up her entire face. "I trust you. Plus, I'm on the pill."

Warmth flows through me at her words. She trusts me. Gaining Ginny's trust was not easy. Especially after how her family treated her growing up. But she trusts me.

"I trust you, too."

"You should. I'm very reliable."

I chuckle before sinking inside her. She moans and her head falls back. I can't resist her elegant neck. I suck and nibble at it as I thrust into her again and again.

Until her nails are clawing at my shoulders. Until her walls are tightening around my cock. Until she moans long and loud.

"Are you ready to come for me, my little librarian?"

"Please," she gasps.

I snake a hand between us to find her clit. I circle it twice before her walls spasm around me.

"Yes!" she shouts as her climax hits her.

Her orgasm sparks mine and I lose all sense of place and time as euphoria hits me. I pound into her until I'm spent and collapse on top of her. I know I should roll off. I'm way too heavy for her. But she wraps her arms around me and holds me close.

"I should move," I mumble.

"No. I feel safe this way. Like the world is far away and nothing can touch me."

"I'll always keep you safe, my love. Always."

"Love you," she mutters.

"I love you, too." I kiss her forehead but realize she's already fast asleep. Good. She needs her rest after today's shit show.

Chapter 28

VIRGINIA

I glide my finger up and down Dylan's right arm. I stop and trace the names of his sisters. Dylan nuzzles my neck.

"You like my tattoos?"

I shrug. "Maybe."

He bites my earlobe before whispering into my ear, "Certainly seemed as if you did when you licked them last night."

I shiver. I did lick every single inch of his tattooed arm last night. I plan to do it again. Soon.

"Have you ever wanted a tattoo?"

I shiver again. Except this time, it's not in anticipation of a night in his arms. He grunts before rolling me until he's hovering over me.

"What's wrong?"

I fast blink. "What do you mean?"

"Ginny."

"Needles freak me out," I blurt out before I can stop myself.

"If those asshole step-brothers of yours tortured you with needles, I'm going to kill them," he growls.

I pet his arm. "It wasn't them."

He cocks a brow.

"Okay. It wasn't entirely them." I'm not sure if I love or hate the way he can read me. I lie. I love it.

"Explain."

"I had bad allergies as a kid and had to get allergy shots every week for two years."

"I'm sorry, my love. Are your allergies better now?"

"Yes, thank you."

"And how did Frick and Frack make it worse?"

"Frick and Frack?"

"Your asshole step-brothers."

I glance away. "The usual. Putting needles in my room. Trying to scare me with them."

"I'm going to kill those assholes."

"You better avoid jail. I'm not one of those reality TV stars who gets married to a murderer."

"I'm not going to kill them." He kisses my nose. "But you can't blame me for wanting to hurt the assholes who hurt the woman I love."

The woman I love. I don't think I'll ever get tired of Dylan saying those words. A bomb of happiness detonates in my body when he does. It starts in my stomach and travels through my body until my fingers are tingling.

I palm his neck and haul him near to meld my lips to his. I sigh when his scent and taste hit me. He doesn't waste any time plunging his tongue into my mouth. His tongue strokes against mine and now my body is tingling for an entirely different reason.

Knock! Knock! Knock!

"No," I groan.

"Ignore it," Dylan growls against my mouth.

"We know you're in there!" Indigo shouts loud enough to wake the entire town of Winter Falls.

I yank my mouth from Dylan's. "She's never going to go away."

"Especially not when the entire band's with her."

"How do you know the entire band's with her?"

He squeezes my hip before rolling out of bed. "They're family."

They're family? What does 'they're family' mean? And why does it mean they're here at my apartment early in the morning?

"I'll get rid of them," Dylan declares before disappearing down the hallway.

I snuggle back into the bed. I rub my legs together in anticipation of all the things Dylan and I can do together in this bed once we're alone again.

"I'm not leaving until I see Virginia with my own eyes!" Indigo yells. "I need to make sure she's okay."

There goes my idea of morning sexy times. I roll out of bed and put on a robe to hide my naked body before venturing into the living room where Dylan's bandmates and Indigo stand staring Dylan down.

The moment I step into the room, Dylan tags my hand and hauls me near. "Sorry. I did try and get rid of them."

Indigo plants her hands on her hips. "I told you. I'm not leaving until I can confirm Virginia's okay."

"You couldn't wait until a decent hour?" Dylan asks.

Cash chuckles. "You're lucky I got her to wait until this morning. She wanted to storm over here last night."

Indigo steps closer. "You're okay?" she whispers her question.

"I'm okay."

"Does this mean I don't get to kick Jett's butt?"

Jett clears his throat and steps forward. "I'm sorry, Virginia."

I debate how to answer. Do I let him off the hook? Or do I let him suffer longer?

"Sorry about what?" Dylan asks before I can finish my internal debate.

"Sorry for scaring you. I didn't think."

Gibson snorts. "Do you ever think?"

"Hey! I'm not stupid."

Fender grunts.

"What?"

"You have to admit it was kind of stupid to enter the horseback combat competition," Gibson says.

"Horseback combat competition?" I ask.

Gibson rolls his eyes. "Mr. Daredevil here decided to enter a jousting competition."

"Except he'd never ridden a horse before," Cash adds.

"Despite the rules of the competition clearly stating it was not for beginner riders," Dylan explains.

Jett crosses his arms over his chest. "I don't understand how this is stupid. So, I forgot to read the competition rules? No one reads those things."

Dylan points at him. "But you refused to withdraw from the competition when you arrived and realized you needed to know how to canter before you can joust."

"What's the big deal? I didn't get hurt."

"But you did get your ass kicked," Fender rumbles.

Gibson waves his phone at Jett. "And I've got the footage to prove it."

"You can't blackmail me with that footage forever. You're not exactly innocent yourself."

"Maybe not, but at least I'm smart enough not to be videoed."

Jett stalks toward Gibson. Before he can reach him, Dylan's there to separate them. "No one will be fighting in Virginia's apartment. Nod if you understand."

Gibson nods and steps back. Jett grunts.

"I'm hungry," Fender says.

"I can make breakfast." I start toward the kitchen but Dylan snatches my wrist to stop me.

"You aren't making breakfast."

"But I'm hungry, too," Gibson pouts.

Dylan points to the door. "Go have breakfast at the diner. There's no need for you to stay here. You've done what you came to do. You checked that Virginia is okay. Jett apologized. We made fun of him. Time for everyone to get out."

Indigo grins. "We'll get out. In fact, we're going swimming. You're coming with."

"Swimming?"

"But I'm not going skinny dipping."

My brow wrinkles. "Why would we go skinny dipping?"

"Apparently everyone in Winter Falls enjoys skinny dipping."

They do? I really need to give up my ban on social media and join the Facebook group. I'm missing out on way too much. Although, I don't need to see any pictures of people swimming naked.

"And it's Dylan and Jett. There's no telling what they'll do."

"Hey, now." Jett holds up his hands. "I'm on my best behavior from now on." Everyone stares at him and he shrugs. "At least when Virginia's around."

Dylan grunts. "You damn well better be or I'm kicking your ass."

"You promised me you'd kick his ass now."

He cracks his knuckles. "Let's do this."

Jett dances away. "Holy cow! Dylan – the peacemaker – is going to kick someone's ass. I would have never bet on this."

"And I wouldn't have bet one of my best friends would scare the crap out of the woman I love."

"Hold on. Woman you love?" Indigo squeals. She rushes to me and grasps my hands while jumping up and down. "We're going to be sisters."

"I don't think you understand how sisters work."

"The band is a family. We're with band members. Ergo, we're sisters."

I don't get a chance to correct her understanding of genetics before she wraps her arms around me.

"I always wanted a sister," she whispers as she rocks me from side to side.

"Me too." Sisters wouldn't have tormented me the way my brothers did.

Dylan pulls me away from her. "And now you have five."

Gibson groans. "Great. Now two of the band members are in love. This shit better not be contagious."

"You don't know what you're missing out on," Dylan says as he smiles down at me.

"I think you're confused. You're the one who's going to be missing out on free p—"

Dylan growls. "Finish that sentence and we have problems."

"It's going to be fun to watch him fall," Cash says.

"I bet he'll screw it up and come crying to us," Indigo adds.

Dylan nods. "Of course, he'll screw it up."

I elbow him. "Be nice."

"The only person I'm required to be nice to is you." He waggles his eyebrows.

"I enjoy it when you're nice to me."

"Let's kick these yahoos out."

Before he can move, the doorbell rings and Fender rushes to answer it. He returns with several plates of food.

"What's going on?" I ask.

"I ordered food," he answers.

"To my house?"

He shrugs. "I told you I was hungry."

"I'm starved," Jett says. "They didn't feed me in jail."

"Didn't you ring Aurora to save you?" Gibson asks.

Jett glares at him. "I don't need Aurora to save me."

"Sure, you don't."

They follow Fender to the kitchen table where he's laying out plates. Gibson snatches a slice of bacon but Fender slaps his hand.

"Didn't anyone ever teach you to share?"

Cash groans as he joins them in the kitchen. "Everyone, behave."

"Happy?" Dylan asks once we're alone in the living room.

More than I can ever express. But I don't want to jinx it. "I am."

"Not annoyed these yahoos messed with our sexy times?"

"Our sexy time window didn't close. We can always open another one."

He smirks. "Hell yeah, we can."

He kisses my nose before going to help the guys with the food.

I scan the group. The man I love is here. The best friend I consider a sister is here. As is her boyfriend who is now a friend as well. And then there are the three bandmates who are doing their best to make me feel welcome.

I didn't only find a man I love. I found a family.

Chapter 29

Surprise attack – unexpected and scary as hell

VIRGINIA

Dylan hauls me into his arms. "I feel bad leaving you."

"You're not leaving me, leaving me. You're going away for one night."

I don't want him to go anywhere, but this is what I signed up for when I fell in love with a rockstar. Now is not the time for my stage five clinger tendencies to engage.

"I still feel bad."

It's probably wrong how much I'm enjoying him feeling bad. But him feeling bad shows he cares, he truly cares.

"You won't be gone long," I remind him. "You'll be home tomorrow."

"I wish I could send Gibson or Jett in my place but Cash and I always do the promo for our new music."

"With good cause." I'm well aware of how much a trouble-maker Jett is and Gibson doesn't seem to be far behind him.

Dylan scowls. "I'm sorry about Jett. I promise he's a good guy. An idiot. But a good guy."

I pat his chest. "I know."

And I do. Not only did Jett apologize in front of the entire band, which couldn't have been easy, but he pulled me aside later to apologize in private. He was nervous and fidgeting as he promised to never prank me again. It was sweet and cute.

"Will you be okay on your own?"

Now it's my turn to scowl. "I'm not weak."

He kisses my nose. "You're far from weak, my love. You're the strongest person I know."

He's wrong. I'm not very strong. Getting stronger? For sure. But the strongest person he knows? Not hardly.

"I'll be fine. Indigo and I are getting together to watch a movie."

"Good."

"Come on Loverboy, time to go," Cash calls from where he's waiting by his car.

"I'll see you tomorrow, Ginny." Dylan's lips meet mine for a brief kiss before he picks up his backpack and strolls to the car.

I watch as they drive away. My stomach gurgles but I place a hand on it and tell it to calm down. It's only one day. Barely twenty-four hours. He'll be back tomorrow morning.

I check my watch. Uh oh. I need to hurry if I don't want to be late to open up the library. I start to walk toward Main Street. I make it two blocks before my phone pings with a message.

Dylan: Miss me yet?

Me: Who's this?

Dylan: Ha! Ha! See if I get you a last-minute present at the airport because I forgot to buy you something in San Diego.

Me: Let me guess. A San Diego Zoo t-shirt with a panda on it.

Dylan: Pandas are cute.

Me: Pandas poop more than 100 times a day.

Dylan: Gross. No stuffed panda for you.

Me: At the library, need to open up.

Dylan: Have a good workday, my love.

Me: Love you.

I stuff my phone in my pocket and unlock the library. I'm setting my purse down on the circulation desk before I realize how easy it was to write love you to Dylan. I've never told a man I've loved him before but with Dylan, I can't seem to stop myself. The man has me – and my heart – completely ensnared.

The day at the library passes quickly. Since the summer holiday began the library is busy with kiddy activities. Five minutes before closing, Indigo arrives.

"What are you doing here? I thought we were meeting at your house?"

She grins. "School's out of session and Cash is gone. I'm bored."

I stare at her. "You're bored or Dylan told you to help me lock up?"

She shrugs. "Dylan might have suggested – strongly – that I help."

I shake my head. "That man."

"You love him."

I roll my eyes. "Of course, I love him. Have you seen him?"

"He's cute but he can't compare to my sexy Cash."

I'm not getting into a discussion about who's sexier – Cash or Dylan – with the woman who's been in love with Cash since she was a teenager.

"Let's lock up. I'm starving," I say instead.

Once the library is closed down, we leave and amber down Main Street toward the house Indigo shares with Cash.

I sigh as we climb the stairs to the porch. I would love to own this house. I can imagine evenings spent on the porch swing reading while Dylan plays his guitar next to me. And – some day – watching our kids run around the yard while we barbeque out back.

Indigo snaps her fingers in front of me. "Where did you go?"

"Just daydreaming."

She smiles. "I love how happy you are."

"I am. I really am."

"Let's go eat a ton of junk food and watch a silly movie to celebrate."

I giggle as she leads me into the house.

It's not long before we're settled on the sofa with a bottle of wine and a platter of nachos watching a romantic comedy.

"Ugh." I groan. "This heroine is too stupid to live."

When Indigo doesn't respond, I glance over at her to discover her sound asleep. I switch off the television and cover her with a blanket before tiptoeing out of the house.

It's still light out as I leave Indigo's home. It's barely a five-minute walk to my apartment building, but I'm in no hurry. It's a beautiful June evening. Thanks to years of allergy shots, I can smell the grass and blooming flowers. Maybe I shouldn't hate needles as much as I do.

I'm nearly at my building when I hear feet pounding my way.

"Virginia? Virginia Hale?"

I glance over my shoulder with a smile ready to greet whoever it is, but the smile dies on my face when I realize it's not one person. It's a whole swarm of people. Assuming paparazzi are actual people. I have my doubts.

"Are you dating Dylan from *Cash & the Sinners*?"

"How long have you been dating?"

"Is the band finished with their album?"

"What's the big announcement they're going to make tonight?"

I don't have time to answer any questions or even say 'no comment' as the questions keep coming – rapid fire style.

Click! The light from the camera nearly blinds me. I hold a hand over my eyes as I blink to regain focus.

I don't get a chance. *Click! Click! Click!* Several cameras are aimed at me and snapping away.

I scan the area to find someone who will help me get rid of these pests. The people of Winter Falls do not approve of the press messing with their residents. But I can't see anything beyond the crowd in front of me. I push onto my tiptoes but it doesn't help any. I'm surrounded and cut off from any possible help.

"I-I-I…" I stutter as the crowd seems to close in on me and fear grips me. They're too close! I need to get away.

I whirl around toward the apartment door but the path is blocked by more paparazzi. Oh god. I'm never going to make it. I'm going to die here on the ground surrounded by these vultures.

You're the strongest person I know.

No, I'm not, Dylan. I'm scared out of my mind and all alone out here.

You're the strongest person I know.

I straighten my shoulders. Despite the fear clinging to every pore of my body, I won't be weak. I won't let these a-words see how much they bother me. How much they scare me.

"Let me through," I manage to say through gritted teeth.

When no one moves, I decide to take matters into my own hands. I shove my way through the crowd toward the door. Every touch from another body makes my skin crawl but I'm not stopping.

By the time I make it to the door, I'm gasping for breath and sweat is rolling down my back. But I'm here. I'm at the door.

My hand shakes as I fit the key in the lock.

"Don't run away!"

"We only have a few questions!"

"Come on, Virginia. Help us out here."

I ignore the shouts and concentrate on fitting the key in the lock. I can do this. The key finally slips into the lock and I hurry to open the door. I'm afraid they'll follow me inside but they don't.

But I'm not safe yet. I won't be safe until I'm locked in my apartment with Dylan.

Dylan! I need to phone Dylan. He'll help.

I run up the stairs to my second floor apartment. This lock is much easier to work. Once I'm inside, I lock the door behind me and collapse against it fighting for air.

I dig my phone out of my purse and dial Dylan. The phone rings and rings and rings, but he doesn't pick up. When his voicemail engages, I end the call before dialing once again.

I don't know how many times I do this, but he doesn't answer any of my calls. I message him instead.

Me: Where are you, Dylan?

Me: I need you, Dylan.

Chapter 30

Break – what you take when you're a chicken

DYLAN

"Calm down, man. I'm sure she's fine," Cash says.

I glare at him. "She's not answering her messages and she's not picking up her phone. She's not fine."

Damn it! I failed Ginny. She needed me and I wasn't there for her.

"Have you heard from Indigo?"

He hands me his phone since he's driving. "Check the messages."

I scroll through his phone. "Nothing."

He frowns. "She promised to message before she went to bed."

Before I have a chance to ask him, he increases our speed until we're flying through the Colorado countryside on our way back to Winter Falls. We were supposed to return tomorrow morning but after I read Ginny's messages and couldn't reach her, I insisted we leave directly after our interview.

We don't speak for the rest of the journey. I'm too busy imagining a million doomsday scenarios to make conversation.

We reach the border of Winter Falls and zoom past a cop car. "Cop."

"No worries," Cash says. "It's Peace. My brother won't arrest me."

I'm still shocked Cash has six half-brothers in Winter Falls. It's the entire reason we ended up here. He was orphaned at seventeen with no family to take him in. And now he has a parcel of brothers plus their partners and children.

The blue lights flash on the police vehicle but Cash doesn't stop until we reach the apartment building. I jump out of the car and rush to the door.

"I'm sorry," Peace calls.

I stumble to a stop. "You're sorry?" I stalk toward him. "What exactly are you sorry for?"

He holds up a hand. "I may be Cash's brother, but I'm still a police officer."

I fist my hands. "What are you sorry for?"

"We had an incident with paparazzi today."

Fucking paps. "What kind of incident?"

"They swarmed the apartment building waiting for Virginia."

"How the fuck did they know about Virginia?" Don't get me wrong. I'm not ashamed to be dating Ginny, but it's none of the world's business who I date.

Peace shrugs. "I assume someone from town told them."

"And once we find out who it is, we'll be dealing with them," Sage says as she joins us with the rest of the gossip gals behind her.

"What happened? Was Ginny hurt?"

My heart nearly stops. Ginny can't be hurt. I know I failed her but she has to be okay.

"We think she's fine, but she's not answering her door," Clove says.

Cayenne holds up a casserole dish. "We wanted to bring her some comfort food."

"And check on her," Feather adds.

"I appreciate it, ladies." And I do. But where the hell were they when the paps were here?

I run a hand down my face. *No fair, Dylan.* I'm her protector. I'm the one who should have been here. No blaming other people to avoid my own guilt.

"I need to check on her," I say and turn away.

"Don't forget the casserole." Cayenne shoves it into my hands.

I hurry into the apartment building and up the stairs to Ginny's apartment. I don't bother knocking on the door. I use my key to unlock it and barge inside.

The living room and kitchen are empty so I run down the hallway to her bedroom. I try to push the door open but it doesn't budge.

"Ginny! Are you in there?"

"Dylan! Dylan, is that you?"

"Open the door, my love."

I hear shuffling before the door opens a smidge. Her chest of drawers is blocking the opening but I'm not waiting. I climb over the piece of furniture until I can reach Ginny and pull her into my arms.

"I'm so sorry, my love." I rock her back and forth as she clings to me. She sniffles and my t-shirt gets soaked as she cries. "I should have been here. I should have made sure you were safe."

"I'm safe now." She hiccups. "With you."

"You're always safe with me."

I pick her up and carry her to the bed. I lay her on it and notice it's completely stripped. "Where are your blankets?"

She points to the closet. I open the door to find she made a bed for herself on the floor. She must have been terrified and hiding in the fucking closet.

I hang my head. This can't happen again. I can't fail her again.

I grab the blankets and cover her with them before crawling into bed with her and cuddling her close.

"I'm sorry."

She sniffs. "It's okay."

"Don't do that."

"Do what?"

"Pretend everything is fine when you were hiding in your closet terrified."

"Thanks for reminding me of what a wimp I am."

I pinch her chin and force her to meet my gaze. "You're not a wimp. Those paps can be terrifying. Have you forgotten what happened to Princess Diana?"

Her eyes widen with fright. Way to scare the woman you love, asshole.

"Forget I said anything. Are you okay now? Why didn't you answer my calls?"

"My phone died and I didn't want to abandon my cocoon to find a charger."

"We're buying extra chargers and putting them in every room in the house," I declare.

"Whoa. Slow down. This is my home. My apartment."

"And you're mine to protect."

She scowls and opens her mouth – probably to remind me of how crappy of a protector I am – but I place a finger over her mouth to stop her.

"I know I failed you today, but I won't fail you again."

She shoves my finger away. "You didn't fail me."

I lean my forehead against hers. "I did, but it won't happen again. Promise. We need to get you an alarm system and maybe a bodyguard when I'm gone since Fender can't keep a promise. How do you feel about dogs?"

"I don't want a bodyguard or an alarm system."

"But you'll accept a dog?"

"I'm serious, Dylan. You need to slow down. Take a breath." Her brow furrows. "Maybe we should take a break."

"What? You're breaking up with me?"

"I didn't say I was. I said we should take a break."

"What's the difference?"

"This is moving too fast," she says instead of answering my question.

"Too fast? I thought you were okay with fast. In fact, you promised to become a stage-five clinger."

I'm joking but she doesn't smile.

"Ginny," I plead. "Don't do this."

"It's a break. Not the end."

I don't believe her. A break is the beginning of the end and we both know it.

"I love you. You love me. We belong together." I'm begging now and I don't fucking care. I can't lose her. She's my sun, my stars, my everything.

"I do love you, but I need time."

"Time for what?"

She motions to the dresser still blocking the door. "Time to figure out how to love a rockstar. Time to figure out if I can handle being the partner of a rockstar."

"I'm not a fucking rockstar," I growl. "I'm Dylan Mitchell. The man you love."

She smiles up at me but it doesn't reach her eyes. "You're also Dylan Mitchell the lead guitarist for *Cash & the Sinners*."

"I'll give up the band."

My words should shock me, but they don't. It's been a grueling ten years of recording an album every year and being on the road ten to eleven months out of the year. I've barely seen my family for a decade.

I certainly don't need to work for the money. I've got enough for the both of us for the rest of our lives and to set our children up after we're gone.

She clutches my t-shirt. "You are not giving up the band for me. I'm not Yoko Ono."

"I always thought the world was too harsh on her."

"I'm serious, Dylan no middle name Mitchell. You are not quitting the band you love for me."

I tuck a strand of hair behind her ear. "I love you more."

"Promise me."

"I promise I love you more than the band."

If those daggers in her eyes were real, I'd be dead now. "Not what I meant and you know it."

I rub a hand down my face. "What am I supposed to do? I can't let you go. You're the love of my life. The woman I've been searching for."

Tears well in her eyes but she blinks them away before they can fall. "Give me time. I need time."

"Will we be in touch during this 'time'?"

She shakes her head. "Giving me time means I need to figure things out on my own."

"Can I at least phone you to check up on you?"

"I don't think it's a good idea."

"I will message you once a day and you will respond. That's my final offer."

"I didn't realize this was a negotiation."

"Ginny, please. I need to know you're safe."

She blows out a breath. "Okay. Fine. One message a day. But no more. No standing behind your apartment door waiting for me to leave and then entering the hallway to 'bump' into me."

I scowl. "How did you know what I planned to do?"

She rolls her eyes. "What do you think I did before we got together?"

"Virginia Hale, were you stalking me?"

"You enjoyed it."

I smile. "I did."

The light-heartedness bleeds out of her eyes. Shit. I'm not going to change her mind. Not right this minute at least. And I'm not pushing her. She needs to come to her own decision in her own time.

But I hate this. I hate this more than anything else I've experienced up until now and Gibson has projectile vomited on me during a concert while I was playing my favorite guitar. It's impossible to get the smell of puke out of the soundhole.

"Okay." I lift Ginny so I can stand. "Do you want me to get Indigo over here for tonight? Otherwise, I'll sleep on the sofa."

She opens her mouth to protest but I hold up a hand to stop her. "I'll agree to give you space but I'm not leaving you alone tonight after what happened."

"I'll message Indigo."

Those words stab into my heart. She doesn't want me near. Fuck. I screwed this all up.

"I'll wait in the living room for her."

At her nod, I stalk to the door. I make quick work of moving the dresser back to its place before leaving the room. I don't look back. I can't. Seeing Ginny sitting in her bed looking lost and alone will break my heart.

I rub a hand over my chest. Who am I kidding? My heart is already breaking.

Chapter 31

Dylan

I don't bother knocking at the house Fender is sharing with Gibson and Jett. I barge inside and the door hits the wall with a bang. Gibson and Jett glance over from where they're sitting in the living room playing a videogame.

I don't bother to greet them. "Where is he? Where's Fender?"

"Is Virginia okay?" Jett asks. "We heard what happened."

"And where were you?"

"We went to her apartment but she wouldn't answer the door and she wasn't answering her phone, so we called Peace."

"You called a cop?"

"Hell, yeah. It's Virginia."

"You've changed your tune."

Jett stands and walks toward me with his palms up. "How many times do you want me to apologize for scaring her? I'm fucking sorry, okay? She's forgiven me. Why can't you?"

Because I can't get the image of her cowering underneath her desk trembling with fright out of my mind. And now I have to add the image of her hiding in her closet alone and afraid, thinking I don't care about her.

I blow out a breath. "I didn't come here to confront you. Where's Fender?"

"Right here," he grumbles from behind me.

I stalk to him. "Where were you? You promised me you'd watch over her."

"He was too busy playing with our neighbor, Leia, to watch over Virginia," Gibson taunts.

Fender growls. "Leave Leia out of it. She has nothing to do with this."

"Except if you weren't obsessed with her, you would have been watching out for Virginia the way you promised," Jett says.

I get in Fender's face. He's a few inches taller and more than a few inches wider than me but I don't give a flying fuck. He's going down for what happened.

"You promised you'd look out for Virginia."

"I'm sorry, man. I thought she was safe at Indigo's house. Indigo promised to message me when Virginia left, but she never messaged."

"It's past midnight. You didn't think to check on her this whole time?"

"I did check on her. Who do you think told these yahoos Virginia was in trouble?"

"I don't care about the hooligans. I didn't entrust the woman I love's safety to them." I stab my finger into his chest. "I entrusted it to you."

He nods. "You did. If it will make you feel better, go ahead and hit me."

"Whoa!" Gibson shouts. "We're not supposed to be hitting each other."

"You hit Jett all the time."

"Because he deserves it. Fender doesn't deserve it."

"What happened to 'he ignored Virginia' to play hide the snake with Leia?"

Fender growls. "Do not bring Leia into this."

"Fine. I won't bring Leia into this, but I will give you the punch you deserve."

I retreat a few steps and fist my hands.

The door flies open and Cash rushes into the house. "No fighting."

I point to Fender. "He agreed I can punch him."

"No one's punching anyone. You're not taking your anger about Virginia dumping you out on Fender."

I glare at him. "Ginny didn't dump me."

"Which is why Indy is at Virginia's house comforting her while she cries her eyes out."

My heart clenches in my chest. Ginny's crying her eyes out? Why did she say she needs to slow things down if it pains her? Why won't she let me comfort her?

Because you didn't protect her when she needed it most, asshole. Thank you, subconscious, I'll handle things from here.

Jett shoves me. "What did you do? Did you hurt her?"

"I didn't hurt her."

Gibson crosses his arms over his chest. "Why is she crying if you didn't hurt her?"

Jett glares at me. "Asshole. Did you break up with her for freaking out when the paps came after her?"

Fender growls. "It was her first encounter with the paps. Of course, it scared her."

"I know." I fucking hate it, but I know.

"Why the hell did you break up with her then?"

"I didn't break up with her."

"You didn't?" Cash asks. "I'm confused."

I blow out a breath and admit, "Ginny's worried she doesn't have what it takes to love a rockstar."

"Bullshit. Virginia's strong," Jett says.

"I know. I told her as much, but she thinks she's weak with how she reacted to the paps."

"From what Peace told me, your girl was anything but weak," Cash says.

I know Ginny's not weak. "What did Peace say?"

"She didn't answer any of their questions and when they wouldn't let her pass, she pushed her way through and got herself to safety in the apartment building."

"That's my girl." Pride fills me. I keep telling Ginny she's the strongest person I know. She doesn't believe me, but I'll keep telling her until she does. I just need to get over this 'I need space'-bullshit first.

"What happened? Why are you here beating up Fender instead of with your girl?" Cash asks.

Fender grunts. "As if."

I run a hand through my hair and pull on the ends. "She wants space. Whatever the fuck that means."

Jett glares at me. "What did you do to her?"

My shoulders fall and I collapse on the sofa. "I couldn't answer my phone when she rang in a panic about the paps. We were in the middle of the interview. I assumed she was fine. I thought Fender had her."

"The offer to hit me still stands."

Hitting Fender isn't the solution. Will it make me feel good? Hell, yeah. But it won't solve my current problem – how to convince Ginny I'm worth the risk. That my being a rockstar isn't a liability. That I can and will protect her in the future.

"What am I going to do?"

"We can play truth or punch until you figure it out," Cash suggests.

Truth and punch is an asinine game he plays with his brothers when one of them screws up.

"I'm not fielding questions from you lot and letting you punch me when I refuse to answer."

He grins. "Don't forget drinking a shot for each question."

"Getting drunk is not the solution."

"What?" Gibson gasps. "Getting drunk is always the solution."

Damn it. I know he's drinking too much. I know it's becoming a problem. But I don't have time to deal with it now. Shit. I'm a sucky boyfriend *and* a sucky friend.

Jett slaps Gibson upside the head. "How is drinking going to help Dylan get Virginia back?"

Gibson shrugs. "Shots open up the mind to the possibilities of the world."

"I think you mean shots make women's panties drop," Jett grumbles.

Cash leans back in his chair. "There's an easy solution here."

Easy? I cock my eyebrow. Nothing about this situation is easy.

"Do a grand gesture."

"A grand gesture?"

"You know. Some over the top gesture to show her you love her and will always be there for her."

I throw a pillow at him. "I know what a grand gesture is."

He chuckles as he catches the pillow. "Didn't sound as if you did."

Jett rubs his hands together. "This is a good idea. What shall we do? Perform in the middle of Main Street for her?"

"Why do you assume there's a 'we'?"

"Virginia's a member of the family. We're all invested in getting her back in the fold."

The rest of the band nods and some of the strain on my chest releases. My bandmates are assholes ninety-nine percent of the time, but the other one-percent? It makes up for everything.

"Thanks, guys, but I think I need to go this one alone."

Gibson scrunches his nose. "You certain? You two haven't been together long and she's already claiming to need 'space'."

"When you fall in love, I'm going to give you so much shit."

"Good thing I am never falling in love."

I snort. "Some woman is going to come along and knock you on your ass so hard you won't know how to use your legs, let alone how to stand."

Fender grunts. "I'd pay to see that shit."

"No need to pay, big guy. We'll have free seats," Cash says.

I rub a hand down my face. "This is amusing but I still don't know how to win Ginny back."

"What does she want?" Cash asks.

"Yeah." Jett nods. "What does she want most in this world?"

"Figure it out and give it to her," Fender says.

There is one thing I know she wants most in this world. One thing I can give to her. I smile as I begin to form a plan.

Watch out, Ginny. You can't get away from me that easy. I finally found the woman I love more than life. And I am not letting you go.

Chapter 32

Mistake – when you let the man you love go because you're afraid

VIRGINIA

I listen as Dylan opens the door and lets Indigo inside. The door closes and Dylan's gone. He left me. Tears burst from my eyes.

I knew this relationship was destined to fail. I knew I should have kept my heart safe from Dylan. I'm such an idiot. A rockstar and a small town librarian? We were doomed before we began.

I cuddle Harry to my chest and crawl under the covers.

"Virginia?" Indigo peers into the room. "Can I come in?" I don't answer. I'm too busy crying my eyes out. "I have casserole."

My stomach rumbles in response. It doesn't care I'm heartbroken. It wants food.

"What kind of casserole?"

The mattress dips as she sits next to me. "You're going to have to come out of there to find out."

I sniff. I smell cheese and pepperoni. My mouth waters. I love cheese.

I lift the corner of the blanket to peek out. Indigo's sitting on the bed with a large casserole dish in her lap. She holds out a spoon to me. "Hungry?"

I snatch the spoon from her. "Starved." I sit up and place Harry in my lap before digging in.

"Virginia?" someone hollers from the hallway.

I freeze. "Who else is here? If you brought the gossip gals with you, I'm going to eviscerate you with this spoon." I brandish the utensil at her as if it's a sword.

"Who do you think baked the casserole? It wasn't me."

"Harry." I nudge my hedgehog. "Attack Indigo." He doesn't budge. "Typical. You get the zoomies whenever I'm alone but now when I need you? Nothing."

"I promise I'm not a gossip gal," the same woman calls from the hallway.

"It's Leia," Indigo admits.

"I'm sorry." Leia sticks her head in the bedroom. "I was with Fender when the whole thing went down with those vultures. I wanted to check on you, but it was late. Then, Indigo showed up at my house and dragged me along."

"Because you're going to be our new best friend."

Leia's eyes widen at Indigo's declaration. I don't blame her. Indigo can be overly assertive. But Leia isn't shy the way I am. She fists her hands at her hips and glares at Indigo.

"What if I don't need any new best friends?"

Indigo rolls her eyes. "Save it. I know you're new to town and haven't had a chance to meet many people yet."

"Because my boss is a fricking slave driver," Leia mutters.

"Are you going to stand in the hallway all night? You're supposed to be bringing the wine."

Leia holds up a bottle of red and some glasses before joining us on the bed. "Don't tell Isla we're eating and drinking in bed. She'll never let me hear the end of it."

"Who's Isla?" I ask around a mouth full of pizza casserole.

Leia's smile lights up her face. "My daughter."

I open my mouth to ask her about her daughter but Indigo holds up a hand to stop me. "No."

"No?"

"No. We're here to sort you out."

"Sort me out?"

"Do you have to repeat everything I say? You're worse than my fourth graders."

"You're not making any sense."

She raises her eyebrows. "I'm not making any sense? Me?" She taps her chest with her spoon causing marinara sauce to stain her t-shirt.

"Yes. You."

"You're the one who doesn't make any sense." She points her spoon at me and sauce flies off it onto my blanket. I nab the spoon from her.

"I have no idea what you mean."

"Why in the world did you break up with Dylan? You've loved him as long as I've loved Cash."

"One, I didn't break up with Dylan. Two, I haven't loved him since high school. And, three, how do you know anything?"

"Everyone knows," Leia answers and I focus on her. She shrugs. "What? They do."

I drop the spoons to bury my face in my hands. "How can the entire town know about me and Dylan? The man barely left my apartment five minutes ago."

"Good news travels fast. Bad news travels faster," Indigo says as she rubs my back. "What happened?"

"The paparazzi descended on me."

"I heard. I'm sorry. I should have made sure you got home safe."

I wave away her apology. "It's not your fault."

"But it is Dylan's fault?"

"No, I don't blame Dylan."

"Then, why did you dump him?"

"I didn't dump Dylan." I huff. "Maybe Dylan dumped me."

Leia snorts and I glare at her. "Sorry, but the man who let us into your apartment did not dump you. He was devastated."

I clutch my chest. "Dylan was devastated?"

She nods. "Completely undone."

"He thinks I blame him for what happened with the vultures."

Indigo nudges me. "Do you blame him?"

"I don't blame him."

"But?" she pushes.

I blow out a breath. "But I couldn't get ahold of him when it happened. He didn't answer his phone or his messages. I probably rang him five hundred times." I shake my head. "I needed him and he wasn't there."

Indigo wraps an arm around my shoulders and I lay my head on her shoulder. "Virginia, best friend of mine, this is what you signed up for when you fell in love with a rockstar. They're not always available. They have concerts and tours and interviews and the list goes on and on."

"Which is why I told Dylan I need a break."

"I can't believe you. You've been obsessed with him for years and at the first hurdle, you bail. I thought more of you, Virginia."

"Hey," Leia says. "Be nice. She's hurting. This couldn't have been an easy decision for her."

"It's my job as best friend to point out when my friend is being an idiot."

"Great," Leia mumbles. "Can I decline the friend offer?"

"Nope. You're stuck with me."

"Awesome."

"Stuck together forever." She squeezes my shoulders. "The same way Dylan and Virginia will always be together."

"Did you forget I told Dylan I need a break?" I ask.

"I'm ignoring it since it's stupid."

I shove her away from me. "I'm not stupid."

"You don't have to be stupid to make a stupid decision."

"How is needing a moment to catch my breath a stupid decision?"

She grasps my hands. "Because this is when you should be holding onto Dylan. The paps scared the daylights out of you. Hold onto the man who makes you feel safe. Who gives you security."

"But he wasn't there."

"I'm here." She nods to Leia. "She's here. The rest of the band is here. You're not alone."

I frown.

"And do you know why you're not alone?"

"Because you're a barnacle and I can't get rid of you."

"Yes, but also the band has adopted you. They're not leaving you alone. In fact…"

She pauses and I about lose my mind. "In fact what?"

"They're taking shifts in the parking lot to make sure none of the paps return."

My mouth gapes open. "They're patrolling the parking lot?"

"All because Dylan loves you and wants you to be safe whether you two are on 'a break' or not."

Holy cow. Dylan didn't give up on me? He didn't stop protecting me after I told him we needed to slow things down?

My heart pounds in my chest. I love that man. Oh, how I love that man. But what about the next time I need him and he isn't around? Can I handle it?

With Indigo and Leia and the band behind me, maybe I can.

Leia sighs. "If I had a man willing to go all out for me, I'd hold onto him."

"Don't worry. Your turn is next." Indigo winks at her.

She holds up her hands. "I don't want a turn. I'm a single mom with a more than full-time job. I don't have time for 'a turn'."

Indigo grins. "Too bad because the gossip gals have their sights set on you."

"I'm not worried."

"Famous last words," Indigo mutters before focusing on me. "Now, what are you going to do?"

I don't know. I want to be with Dylan. I love him more than anything in the world. But I don't know if I'm strong enough. Whenever I get scared, I revert back to a frightened little mouse.

"Don't you dare say you aren't strong enough to love a rockstar." Indigo pats my thigh. "You handled the paps perfectly today."

I feel my face heat. "And then I fell apart when I got into my apartment."

"It was your first encounter. Remind me to tell you sometime about what happened during my first encounter with the vultures."

"Do I want to know?"

"The point is it gets easier. And Winter Falls won't make you deal with them on your own."

"Oh. I forgot." Leia hands me a card. "This was with the casserole."

I open the card and read it out loud. "We're sorry we missed the paparazzi invading Winter Falls. We won't let it happen again. You have our word. Signed, The Gossip Gals."

"You should frame that. I bet those ladies don't apologize very often."

"I messed up, didn't I?"

I thought I was all alone. I thought I had to handle everything by myself. But I don't. Even when Dylan isn't there, I'm not alone. He made sure I'm not.

"What am I going to do?" I wail and tears begin to well in my eyes.

Indigo taps my cheek. "First of all, no crying. Second of all, easy peasy."

I sniff and suck the tears back into my eyes. "Easy peasy?"

"It's grand gesture time, baby."

"What kind of grand gesture could I possibly do? Dylan has all the money in the world. He doesn't need anything."

"It's not about what he needs. It's about showing him you love him, you choose him."

"How do I …"

My question trails off when I realize I have the perfect idea to show Dylan how much I love him.

Chapter 33

Surprise – when someone gives you the thing you expect least in the world

DYLAN

I pace the hallway between my apartment and Ginny's. Where is she? She finished work and closed up the library over two hours ago. And she's not at any other establishment in Winter Falls. Trust me. I know. I've had all of them checked.

I'm frantic. The band is frantic.

Ginny is missing.

I dig out my phone and dial Peace.

"You can't report her missing," he says upon answering. "No matter how many times you call and bother me." I may have called him a few times already.

"But she is missing. No one knows where she is."

"Someone must know where she is. Have you asked all of her friends?"

"Indigo isn't answering her phone. Her boss said she left work at the usual time. And no one in town has seen her."

"I'll hop in a patrol car and drive around again but I'm certain she'll turn up soon."

"Easy for you to say. It's not the woman you love who's missing."

He sighs. "I'd put a tracker on Olivia if she let me."

A tracker? Good idea. I can put a gizmo in a necklace or a ring. Yeah, a ring's better. Although, there's no way Ginny will accept a ring from me at the moment. Her behavior over the past few days – sneaking in and out of the apartment building to avoid seeing me – doesn't exactly scream *buy me a ring!*

Good thing for me, she's not great at sneaking around. Or, at least, I thought she wasn't. Somehow she got away from me today. Damn. I've failed her again.

Maybe I should let her go. I obviously can't keep her safe. She needs a protector. Someone who is always there for her.

"Whatever you're thinking, stop," Peace says and I startle. I forgot we were still connected. "Virginia loves you and things will work out. I promise."

"How the hell can you know that?"

"Did you forget I'm a police officer?"

"Being a police officer doesn't equal knowing the hearts and souls of the residents of the town."

"Give me the phone!" someone shouts. I hear a scuffle in the background.

"Don't make me hit you, young man!"

"I'm not hitting you but you can't steal my phone."

"I'll steal your phone if I want to. I used to change your diapers."

"Fine."

"It's Sage, leader of the gossip gals."

"She's not the leader!"

"Don't you worry. Your Virginia will be home soon."

I don't get a chance to ask her how she could possibly know where Ginny is before she hangs up.

I shove the phone back in my pocket and resume pacing of the hallway. *Think, Dylan. Think.* I have four sisters I helped raise. I should be able to figure this out.

Where did they go when they were hurting and trying to avoid someone? It's no use. Somehow I don't think Ginny's at the beach stuffing her face with ice cream.

She must be somewhere in town. She doesn't have a car. Hold on a minute. She doesn't have a car, but she does have a bike. Maybe she went for a bike ride. This is why no one's seen her. We've been scouring the streets of Winter Falls and she's out on the bike trails.

I rush for my apartment. I'll get the keys to my bike and then I'm finding Ginny.

I hurry into the hallway and start for the stairs only to come to an abrupt halt when Ginny appears in front of me.

I haul her into my arms. "Thank god you're okay."

She sinks into my embrace and I tighten my arms. As long as she's not pushing me away, everything is right in my world.

"Ouch," she squeaks.

I step back and grasp her shoulders. "Where are you hurt? Do we need an ambulance?" I dig my phone out. "Screw the ambulance. Cash will drive faster."

She bats my phone away. "I don't need an ambulance."

"You're in pain. You said ouch." My stomach clenches as another scenario enters my mind. "I didn't hug you too tight, did I?"

"You can never hug me too tight."

I'm confused. I can never hug her too tight but I can push her too fast. What does it all mean? I run a hand through my hair and pull on the ends.

"Are you in pain? Are you hurt? Can I help?"

She pats my chest. "I'm not hurt. You can't help. But I am in a little pain."

No hurt but in pain. "Ah, it's that time of the month. No worries. I can have a period packet ready in minutes. Go rest." I usher her toward her door. "Do you have a heating pad?"

She digs her feet in. "It's not my time of the month." Her cheeks flare with the admission.

"You gotta help me out. I don't know what's wrong. If I don't know what's wrong, I don't know how to fix it."

"You don't have to fix everything."

"If it involves you, I'm fixing it."

"You're also ruining your surprise," she mumbles. When she realizes she spoke out loud, she slaps a hand over her mouth and retreats. "Forget I said anything."

I crowd her until her back is against the wall. I place my hands next to her head to cage her in.

"What surprise?"

She clamps her mouth shut and shakes her head back and forth.

I lean close to whisper in her ear. "What surprise?"

She shivers but she doesn't give in.

I step closer until I can feel the heat of her body. We're not touching but if she heaves a breath, we will be.

"What surprise?"

Her chest rises and those magnificent breasts touch me. I fist my hands to stop myself from reaching for her. She has to make the first move. She's the one who wanted a break. I can't touch her without her permission.

"Ouch."

I freeze. "You are hurt."

I grasp her hand and drag her into my apartment. I get her settled on the sofa before sitting in front of her.

"I know I'm not your favorite person right now. I'm not going to force you to tell me what's wrong. But I'm begging you to please let me call Indigo to help you. I can't stand seeing you in pain."

She scowls at me. "You're determined to ruin your surprise."

"Ginny, my love, I don't give a shit about the surprise. I do give a shit the woman I love is in pain and I can't do anything about it."

"Dang it." She huffs. "I can't keep my grand gesture a surprise if you beg me."

"Grand gesture? Why the hell are you doing a grand gesture?" I'm the one who needs to do a grand gesture. I'm the one who failed her.

Pain flashes in her eyes. "Because I'm an idiot who got scared and pushed you away."

"You're not an idiot. You can never be an idiot."

"You didn't deny I got scared and pushed you away."

I shrug. "We all get scared sometimes. Ask me about the time Joni found a spider in the bathtub one day."

She smiles just the way I intended. "Spiders are creepy."

"I'll fight a battalion of spiders over a group of paparazzi who smell fresh blood any day."

"They scared me."

I can't keep my distance any longer. Not when she's talking about being scared. I cup her chin. "I know they did, but you handled them like a champ. Didn't give them any information and made your way out of there without getting into a fist fight. You deserve a medal."

"And you deserve a woman who doesn't curl up in a blanket fort in her closet because she got swarmed by the press."

I lean forward to kiss her forehead. "I have the woman I deserve. She's sitting in front of me not realizing she's the strongest person I know."

"I want to show you I'm not a mouse."

I scowl. "I know you're not a mouse."

"I did something scary to prove it."

"What did you do? Please tell me you weren't out skydiving or parkour racing with Jett. I know he's your new best friend, but he's a menace."

It irks the hell out of me, but Jett's the only member of the band who's been able to get close to Ginny over the past few days. Ever since the failed prank, Jett has been Ginny's biggest champion.

She shivers. "No skydiving or parkouring. I don't even know what parkouring is."

"It's when…" I trail off when I realize the definition of parkouring is not what's important here. "What did you do?"

"I can't tell you. I have to show you."

"Okay." I lean back and cross my arms. "Show me."

Her cheeks darken. "Can you look away?"

I nod. "Of course."

I turn around to face the front door. Clothes rustle and my blood heats. Is she stripping for me? My cock twitches. He wants to see the show. I keep a tight rein on my hormones as I wait for Ginny to tell me I can look.

She clears her throat. "You can turn around now."

I adjust myself before swiveling on the table to find Ginny sitting topless on my sofa. My blood pounds through my veins. *Yes!* But then I notice there's a bandage over her heart.

"What happened? You are injured! I'll call emergency."

I rush to my feet but she catches my wrist to stop me.

"I'm not injured. This bandage isn't covering a wound. It's covering a tattoo."

I freeze. "A tattoo? But you're afraid of needles."

"I wanted to face my fear of needles to prove to you I'm worthy of being your partner."

I scowl. "You don't have to prove you're worthy of me. You are worthy of me. In fact, you're too good for me."

"Agree to disagree."

I start to argue but I realize this isn't an argument I can win. Not today. It's an argument I have to win day after day until Ginny realizes her worth.

"Are you going to show me the tattoo?"

She bites her bottom lip. "Do you want to see it?"

Is she seriously asking me? "Hell, yeah."

She begins to peel the bandage off. I bat her hands away. "Let me."

As gently as I can, I remove the bandage to reveal the plastic wrap covering the tattoo. "It's a guitar."

"Look closer."

I study the guitar and realize my name is written along the strings. "You got my name tattooed on your heart."

"My heart belongs to you."

At those words, everything is right in the world once again. I don't care if Ginny needs space. She can have it. As long as we end up together, she can have all the space she needs.

"I love you, Virginia Hale."

"And I love you, Dylan Mitchell."

I wrap a hand around her hair and pull her head back before slamming my lips against hers. Her taste hits me and I moan. I've missed her taste. It's only been two days but those two days felt like they lasted five years.

My phone buzzes in my pocket to remind me we need to get moving. I gentle the kiss until I can pull away.

"As much as I want to strip you bare and worship your body to thank you, we don't have time."

"Don't have time? Do you have a previous engagement?"

"*We* have a previous engagement."

She frowns at me. "I didn't make an appointment with you."

I kiss her nose. "I did it for you."

She narrows her eyes on me. She knows I'm up to something, which I obviously am. "What's going on?"

I hold out my hand to her. "Come and find out."

When she doesn't hesitate to fit her hand in mine, my heart swells. I have her back. I have my Ginny back after two days of hell.

I'm not letting her get away from me again. Ever. She's mine. My heart, my soul, my better half.

Chapter 34

Surprise – when someone gives you the thing you want most in the world

Virginia

"Where are we going?" I ask once we exit the apartment building and begin walking down the sidewalk.

Dylan squeezes my hand. "You'll see, my love."

My heart spasms with joy at those words. He still loves me. I didn't lose him for being a big fat scaredy-cat. The tattoo on my chest twinges to remind me I'm not a scaredy-cat. I'm not a mouse. I'm strong. And I can handle loving a rockstar, come what may.

"Can you give me a hint?"

"You're going to love it."

"That's not a hint. That's a prediction."

"Sorry, my little librarian. I'll give you a hint." He winks. "It's in Winter Falls."

"You suck at giving hints. 'In Winter Falls' could mean absolutely anything."

He smirks. "I know."

"If I guess what it is, will you tell me if I'm right or wrong?"

"Yes."

"Is it a bigger basket for my bike?"

"Wrong but we can pick up a new basket if you want one."

I ignore his offer. "Is it a dinner reservation at the brewery?"

"Wrong."

"Is it a new cage for Harry?"

"Not exactly."

Not exactly. I'm getting close. "What do you mean not exactly?"

"I didn't agree to follow-up questions."

"But you're supposed to indicate if I'm right or wrong."

He shrugs. "Sorry. No can do."

I squeeze his hand. "Come on. Give me something."

"Patience is a virtue," he sings.

"And now I know why you're not the lead singer of the band," I grumble.

He barks out a laugh. "Hitting me where it hurts. Ouch."

"You don't sound hurt." I elbow him for good measure.

He pulls a blindfold out of his back pocket. "Will you agree to be blindfolded?"

I cross my arms over my chest and consider his question. The idea of going into a situation blind does not excite me, but this is Dylan. He won't let anything happen to me.

"You better make it worth my while."

He spins me around, places the blindfold on, and ties it in the back. He kisses my neck before whispering in my ear, "I'll make it worth your while over and over again tonight."

I ignore the shiver darting through my system at the feel of his breath on my skin and his voice in my ear. "If this is a sex thing, I'm going to be disappointed."

"My love, I will never disappoint you."

Is he trying to make me combust into flames in the middle of the street in Winter Falls where anyone could be watching? Where anyone is probably watching?

"Come along." He grasps my hand and leads me around the corner.

"Are we there yet?"

"Almost."

We stop a few steps later and he spins me around until I don't know which way I'm facing.

"Is there a pinata? I have to warn you, I'm a competitive pinata player."

He chuckles. "There's no pinata. But good idea for the future."

"Bring it on, guitar boy. Bring it on."

"Close your eyes."

"They're closed."

He moves behind me and removes the blindfold. "Ta-da!"

I open my eyes to discover we're standing in front of a house. It's a Colonial on the same street Indigo lives on.

"What are we doing here?" I can hear people in the backyard. "Is there a party? Did you throw me a surprise party?"

"There is a party, but the party isn't your surprise. The house is."

I gasp. "What?"

"I bought this house for you. For us. For our family."

This can't be happening. I must be dreaming. I pinch myself. "Ouch!"

"This isn't a dream, my love. This is real. I know the thing you want most in the world is a house of your own."

"Not a house. A home," I correct.

"A home." He clears his throat. "But I don't want to pressure you. The house is in your name. If you don't want me to live here with you, I'll understand. I'll do everything in my power to change your mind, but I'll understand."

I whirl around to face him. "Why wouldn't I want you to live here? Do you leave the toilet seat up? Do you throw wet towels on the bathroom floor? Do you leave hair all over the sink after you shave? Do you leave the empty toilet paper roll on and not change it?"

He scratches his chin. "I don't leave the toilet seat up. I can learn to pick up the towels. I know better than to not change an empty toilet roll. There's a slight chance I leave hair in the sink when I shave."

I sigh. "You were this close." I hold up my hand with my index finger and thumb an inch apart. "And then you blew it at the end."

"What if we have his and her sinks in the bathroom?"

My eyes widen. "There are his and her sinks in the bathroom?"

"Not yet but the bathroom off the main bedroom needs a complete gut job." He clears his throat. "Actually, the house needs a ton of work. The bones are good, though."

"The bones are good, though," I repeat.

He holds out his hand. "Are you ready to view your new home?"

"Only if it's *our* new home."

He palms my neck and draws me near. "Are you serious? No more break?"

I snort. "I think the break was over when I undressed for you half an hour ago."

"Technically, you still had your pants on."

I take his hand. "Do you want to discuss semantics or do you want to show me our new home?"

"Is this a trick question? Show you our new home."

As we're walking up the sidewalk, the door flies open and Indigo bursts out. "You have to get in here now."

"We're coming," Dylan says.

"Not you. Virginia."

"What's wrong? Is there a leak? Do we have mice? We can't have mice. Harry will be terrified."

Indigo rolls her eyes. "Doomsdayer. There's no leak or mice, but there is plenty of drama."

"I've had enough drama over the past days for the rest of my life. Leave me out of it."

She waggles her eyebrows. "You won't want to miss this. It's Leia and Fender. They're having a screaming match in your backyard."

"They are?"

Dylan chuckles. "So much for not wanting any drama."

"Oh, please. I know you and the other band members gossip more than the gossip gals."

He lays a hand against my cheek. "Go on. We have the rest of our lives to explore this house and make it into a home. A home our children will grow up in."

"Swoon!" Indigo shouts.

I ignore her. I'm not letting her ruin the moment. No one can ruin this moment. It's perfect. We're perfect. And here I thought I didn't know how to love a rockstar. I got this.

I push up on my toes. "Love you, guitar man," I whisper before kissing him.

"Love you, too, my little librarian." He slaps my bottom. "Now, go on. Get out of here. Find out what's going on and report back."

"Aye, aye, captain."

I kiss him one more time before dashing toward Indigo. She grasps my hand and pulls me into the house. I plant my feet at the threshold and glance over my shoulder at Dylan.

"I didn't say thank you."

"You love me. I don't need any more thanks than that."

I touch my hand to my chest over my new tattoo. "You're stuck with me now."

He looks down at his left arm. Unlike his right, the left arm is completely free of tattoos. "Do you know any good tattoo artists?"

The idea of my name permanently inked on his body has me tugging my hand away from Indigo to return to Dylan.

"I might." I wink. "What do you need it for?"

He pinches my chin. "I want to put the name of my love on my arm so she can trace it with her tongue while I'm buried deep inside her."

I tremble. "I think this is an excellent idea," I gasp out.

"Me too."

His head lowers to mine but before his lips can reach me Indigo shouts, "You guys are worse than me and Cash!" and stomps away.

I burst into laughter and bury my face in Dylan's shoulder. He wraps his arms around me and I snuggle in close to where I want to be. This is where I always want to be.

Chapter 35

Leia – a single mom who doesn't need a childless bass player to tell her how to be a parent

Leia

"Mom!" Isla shouts loud enough for the entire state of Colorado to hear.

I blow out a breath and search for my patience before answering – in a normal voice since my daughter is only one room away – "What?"

"We're going to be late."

I bury my face in my hands. I don't want to go to a party. I have a ton of work to do thanks to my boss. Does the man ever sleep?

Isla rushes into the room. "Mom. Stop stalling."

Since when is trying to finish twenty projects before going to a party stalling? I don't bother explaining to my daughter, though. She's eleven. She doesn't need to know how hard I work to keep a roof over our heads and food on the table. She needs to enjoy life.

I guess we're going to a party.

I shut my laptop and stand. "Are you ready?"

"I was ready an hour ago when you said to be ready in five minutes."

I tweak her nose. "I think someone's exaggerating. Better be careful before your nose grows."

She giggles. "Mom. Pinocchio isn't real."

I wrap an arm around her and lead her out of my office to the front door. She skips as we make our way down the sidewalk.

"Will Fender be at the party?"

At the mention of his name, I can't help myself from glancing at the house next door to where the rockstar lives. Fender Hays, bass player for *Cash & the Sinners*, is sexier in person than he is on the cover of a magazine and he's pretty darn sexy on the cover of a magazine.

Only in person can you experience how tall and broad-shouldered with muscles everywhere he is. Not that I've touched any of his muscles. I wouldn't. I've sworn off men after Isla's dad abandoned us. Plus, Fender's a rockstar. He wouldn't be interested in a single mom.

Unfortunately, Isla is in love with him. She sits and stares out the window waiting for him to make an appearance. I didn't realize how much she missed a father figure until Fender showed up. But Fender is no father figure. He's a rockstar who will leave Winter Falls soon enough.

"Mom." Isla tugs on my hand. "Will Fender be at the party?"

I force my thoughts away from Fender's imminent departure from town and smile down at my daughter. Considering this party is to celebrate Fender's bandmate, Dylan, buying my friend, Virginia, a house, I assume Fender will be there. My tummy warms at the idea of seeing him again. Calm down, I tell it. We've sworn off men, remember?

"Fender will probably be there," I tell my daughter.

"Yes!"

Her pace increases until we're practically sprinting down the sidewalk toward the party.

"Slow down. Hold your horses."

She giggles. "I don't have any horses. I've never even ridden a pony."

Silly me. I had to mention horses. Isla has been begging me to learn how to ride a horse since she was five years old and another kid in her kindergarten class bragged he owned a ranch.

I quickly calculate the cost of a pony ride. Things are financially much better since I started working as Brody Bragg's assistant. We now live in a cute house and the town of Winter Falls is safe and child friendly. Maybe I can swing a pony ride.

I ruffle Isla's hair. "Maybe we can do a pony ride for your twelfth birthday."

Her eyes widen and sparkle with happiness. "We can?"

"I said maybe."

"I'll convince you."

My chest fills with pride at how confident she sounds. All I've ever wanted is for my daughter to become a confident young woman without the typical hang-ups about looks or school or any of the other teenage angsts.

"Hey!" Indigo waves me over when we reach the party. Isla runs to her and jumps into her arms. "How's my favorite eleven-year-old?"

"Eleven and a half," my daughter immediately corrects.

Indigo nods. "My mistake. How is my favorite eleven-and-a-half-year-old?"

Isla giggles. "You're silly."

Indigo's eyes widen. "I'm silly? You're silly." She tickles Isla and my daughter bats her away.

"There she is. The princess of the party," Jett says as he and Gibson join us.

"What do you think of my dress?" Isla twirls around showing off her summer dress.

"It's adorable," Gibson says.

Indigo leans close to whisper to me, "I didn't know Gibson knew the word adorable."

"Shush you. The guys are great with Isla." Which is going to make it difficult when they leave. And they will be leaving soon considering the album they've been recording is now finished. Cash and Dylan announced it on some entertainment news show the other night.

"Fender!" Isla shouts and runs after him.

"What does the big guy have that we don't?" Gibson pouts.

Arms strong enough to lift me up? Shoulders broad enough for me to cry on? A beard I want to dig my fingers into? A chest I want to lick until my mouth goes dry?

Indigo touches the corner of my mouth. "You're drooling."

I snap my mouth shut. "I am not drooling."

She grins. "Yes, you are. This is fun."

I glare at her. "This is not fun. My daughter is growing attached to a man who's leaving town soon."

"What if he doesn't leave town?"

I roll my eyes. "Of course, he's leaving town. The band is done recording."

She shrugs. "Cash isn't going anywhere." She points to the house. "And Dylan isn't going anywhere now either."

Because they've found the women they love here in Winter Falls. Fender is not interested in finding a woman. His stay away vibes are impossible to miss.

I watch as Fender picks Isla up and twirls her around. He smiles and his dimples make an appearance. His grumpy appearance fades away and a man who looks able to rock your world with a crook of his finger appears.

My daughter motions for me to join them but before I can, my phone rings with *The Imperial March*. I groan.

"Can you watch Isla?"

At Indigo's nod, I make my way to the corner of the yard where I can hold a private conversation.

"What's up, boss man?"

Brody responds but I'm not paying attention. How can I when Fender is prowling toward me with his grumpy face?

"Are you listening to me?"

Oops! "Send me an email and I'll get to work on it when I get home."

I hang up as Fender arrives.

"This is a party," he growls.

I gasp. "No? Really? I wouldn't have realized. What with all the people milling around eating and drinking and being merry."

"If you know it's a party, why are you working?"

"I'm not working."

He nods to my phone.

"I answered one call."

He crosses his arms over his chest and those arm muscles bulge with the movement. I never knew you had to be fit to be a bass player before. Now, I'm well aware. Oh, so aware.

"And?"

My gaze flies from his chest to his face. "And what?"

"You not only answered a call, you agreed to work when you get home."

"I don't understand why this concerns you."

He nods to Isla who's laughing hysterically as she runs away from Gibson and Jett who are chasing after her. "You need to be there for your daughter."

I seethe. How dare he? Who does he think he is? I'm Isla's mom. I've been there for her – by myself – since day one. "Are you questioning my parental skills?"

He cocks an eyebrow.

"How dare you?" I stab him in the chest with a finger. Ouch! I pull my hand away and rub my finger. "How dare you? You've known Isla for a hot minute. You don't know anything about being a parent. About staying up all night with your little girl when she has a fever. About worrying yourself sick when she's nervous to start a new school."

"I—"

I hold up a hand. "I don't want to hear it. I'll make sure Isla leaves you alone from here on out."

As I march away, I'm seething. I wouldn't be surprised if there was hot air coming out of my ears. Who the hell does Fender Hays think he is? Telling me how to raise my daughter?

Asshole. This is why I've sworn off men. They're all a bunch of assholes.

Chapter 36

The end – only the beginning

SEVERAL MONTHS LATER

Dylan

I watch Ginny pace the living room for a few minutes before I sigh and stand to go to her. I wrap my arms around her. "Stop."

"Stop? Stop what?"

"Pacing around the living room like you're Harry and it's eight in the evening and we haven't let him out to do the zoomies yet."

"I do not have the zoomies."

"I didn't say you did."

"It sounded as—" She freezes. "Did I hear a car door? I think I heard a car door."

She runs to the front door and flings it open. "They're here. Oh god. They're here." She clutches her chest. "What if they hate me? What if they realize I'm not good enough for you?"

I haul her near. "My family doesn't hate you. You've met them on Zoom calls and they loved you. And if there's anyone who's not good enough for anyone it's me of you."

She snorts. "Says the rockstar to the little librarian."

I rub my nose along hers. "I love my little librarian."

"Mom! They're making out."

"Gross!"

I chuckle. "You good?" She nods. "You ready to meet your nephews?" Another nod.

I whirl her around. "Noah and Elijah meet your Aunt Virginia."

Ginny waves at them. "Hi!"

"Do you play in a rock band like Uncle Dylan?" Noah asks.

"No, I'm a librarian."

Noah's nose wrinkles but Elijah's eyes light up. "Have you read the Percy Jackson books?"

"Of course."

"Which is your favorite?"

"Mom," Noah whines. "Elijah's being boring."

I wrap an arm around his neck and rub my knuckles over his head. "Who's boring now?"

"I had to have two boys. I couldn't have had girls," Janis complains when she steps onto the porch.

I snort. "As if girls are easier to raise."

I notice Ginny wringing her hands together and place a hand on her back in support. She leans into me. I will never get tired of her leaning into me.

"Hi," Ginny says. "It's—"

Janis launches herself at her. "Thank goodness Dylan found you."

"I didn't realize he was lost."

Janis giggles. "You're going to fit in just fine."

"Stop hogging her." Linda elbows Janis out of the way so she can hug Ginny.

I check she's okay before going to help Mom with the suitcases.

"About time you came to help," Mom grumbles with a smile on her face.

"Just making sure Ginny's not overwhelmed with this crazy family."

Mom throws her arms around me. "I'm happy for you."

"Thanks, Mom."

"Now," she says as she releases me, "let's get this car unpacked. I'm ready to put my feet up."

"You should have let me pick you up from the airport," I say as I grab the suitcases.

"Don't be silly. There was no need for you to drive all the way to Denver and back. We were fine."

Mom's always fine, and she never needs help. Or so she says.

"Come and meet Ginny." I nod toward the house where Ginny is surrounded by my four sisters. My two nephews are missing but I'm not surprised. I know how it feels to be outnumbered by a bunch of girls in the family.

Mom rushes toward the house. Ginny notices her, her eyes widen, and she starts wringing her hands again. My little librarian is shy. Her cheeks darken and my pants tighten. A blush on her cheeks never fails to make my cock twitch with excitement. He's addicted to her. As am I.

"Ms. Mitchell," Ginny greets.

"It's Emma. None of this Ms. Stuff," Mom says and gathers Ginny into her arms. She rocks her back and forth. "Welcome to the family, Virginia."

I set the luggage in the foyer before rescuing Ginny from my mom. "You're scaring her."

"How could I be scaring her? Who's afraid of a hug?"

"Who's afraid of Virginia Woolf?" Elijah chuckles at his own joke.

Ginny rolls her eyes. "Not very original."

"Too bad Uncle Dylan's last name isn't Woolf. Then, when you get married, you'll really be Virginia Woolf."

"M-m-married," Ginny stutters.

"Duh. You have to be married to be my aunt," Elijah claims.

Janis squeezes his shoulder. "No, they don't."

"But what about—" Janis slaps a hand over her youngest son's mouth.

"Way to keep a secret," she mutters before ushering him inside. "Let's go find our bedroom."

Ginny follows them. "Let me show you."

"Let's all go," Joni says as she herds Linda and Stevie in front of her.

"But I want to watch this," Stevie protests.

Joni and Linda each grab one arm and drag her away. It's a scene I've witnessed a million times. It never fails to make me smile.

Mom threads her arm through mine. "Are you happy?"

"It's good to see you guys here in person."

"We would have come sooner but someone wanted to finish the house first."

I shake my head. "The place was a construction zone until last week. Trust me. You should be glad you weren't here."

"At least we had our Zoom calls."

She raises an eyebrow and now it's my turn to be nervous considering what I asked her for during our last talk.

"Shall we discuss this in my office?" I ask but don't wait for an answer before leading her down the hallway to the music room.

Mom walks around the room touching my guitars. "I should have known your office would be a music room. You always were playing on that dang guitar your dad gave you for your tenth birthday."

I shrug. "I think it paid off."

"As long as you're happy."

"I am. I never thought I could be this happy."

She removes a small box from her pocket and hands it to me. "This belongs to you."

I flip it open to reveal the diamond ring inside. "I can't believe you kept it."

"It was your grandmother's engagement ring. Of course, I kept it."

"I meant…" I trail off. She knows what I meant. How I expected her to pawn the ring off when we were hurting for money after Dad left.

"Some things are worth sacrificing for."

"They are." All those high school activities I missed out on to ensure my sisters were enjoying their teenage years were totally worth it.

"Virginia is lovely."

I can't help a smile from spreading over my face. "She's my everything."

"I'm glad." A tear slips from her eye and I wipe it away.

"Don't be sad."

"I'm not sad. I'm happy. I'm proud I raised a son who knows the value of a good woman when she's standing in front of him."

I grasp her shoulders. "I do."

She slaps my chest. "Not me, silly. Your Virginia."

"I can know the value of more than one good woman in my life."

"You're a good man, Dylan."

My chest swells at her words. "Thanks to you, Mom. Thanks to you."

The door flies open and Noah and Elijah rush inside. "Uncle Dylan, I want the top bunk. I'm the oldest I should have the top bunk," Noah shouts.

"But I called dibs," Elijah says.

Ginny rushes in behind them. "I'm sorry. I was trying to let you have a moment with your mom."

"No need, my dear," Mom says as she herds the boys toward the door. "Show me this room with bunk beds."

"Is everything okay?" Ginny asks once we're alone again.

"Everything's perfect."

"You sure? Your mom had tears in her eyes."

I draw her into my arms. "She says they were happy tears."

Ginny blows out a breath. "Good. I want your family to enjoy it here. I want them to visit often."

I'm glad since I want the same things. "And you want them to like you."

She shrugs. "There's nothing wrong with wanting your family to like me."

"No, there isn't, my love." Her arms tighten around me. They always do when I call her my love, which is why I do it as often as I can. "Are you happy, my love?"

She leans back to meet my gaze. "I'm so happy, I'm scared."

I tuck a strand of hair behind her ear. "There's nothing to be scared of. I'll always be there to catch you if you fall."

"I know."

I can't resist the lure of her lips. I want her taste of sunshine and summer days in my mouth. I want to breathe in her honey scent.

She sighs the moment our lips touch and I press my tongue into her mouth. I stroke my tongue against hers until her fingernails bite into my shoulders. I growl and draw her closer. Until her breasts strain against my chest.

The door opens behind me, but I ignore it.

"Grandma!" Elijah shouts. "Uncle Dylan and Aunt Virginia are kissing again."

"It's gross," Noah adds.

I can hardly ignore my nephews. No matter how much I want to. I slow the kiss until I'm sipping from Ginny's lips.

"To be continued," I whisper.

"No way, mister. No sexy times with your family in the house."

I smirk. "I'll change your mind."

"You're lucky I love you, Dylan Mitchell."

"I am. I'm the luckiest man in the world. I love you, Ginny."

There's a crash somewhere outside the room and I sigh. "Welcome to Mitchell family life."

Her eyes light up. "Thank you for giving me everything I could ever want."

"The best is yet to come, my love. The best is yet to come."

D. E. Haggerty
Love and Laughter in Every Chapter

About the author

D.E. Haggerty is an American who has spent the majority of her adult life abroad. She has lived in Istanbul, various places throughout Germany, and currently finds herself in The Hague. She has been a military policewoman, a lawyer, a B&B owner/operator and now a writer.

www.ingramcontent.com/pod-product-compliance
Lightning Source LLC
LaVergne TN
LVHW041458170726
843492LV00005B/1288